KENNETH SCHNEYER

THE LAW & THE HEART

FOREWORD BY LIZ ARGALL

STILLPOINT/PROMETHEUS

Stillpoint Digital Press
Mill Valley, California
StillpointDigitalPress.com

FIRST EDITION

Published in the United States of America

For the publication history and copyright information of individual stories, see Publication History, page xi.

Book & cover design by David Kudler, StillpointDigitalPress.com

10 9 8 7 6 5 4 3 2

Print ISBN 978-1-938808-22-7
Ebook ISBN 978-1-938808-23-4

For Janice,
without whom none of it
would have happened

Contents

Foreword

Liz Argall

Dear friend, I want you to buy this book because it is tender, thoughtful, funny, you'll make friends with some beautiful new characters, and it might change the way you view contracts and seemingly bland paperwork forever. Go ahead and buy it, we'll be here when you get back.

When you do, you will be entertained by stories that explore the definitions of humanity, time travel, the construction of identity, intellectual property, artificial intelligence, library fines, paying to hang out in someone else's body (whether they like visitors or not), domestic violence, linguistics, parenting, intergalactic multilateral agreements in a relativistic universe, aging, memory, and just how sweet sex can be when you been learning each other's preferences for over twenty years.

Dear friend, thank you for buying Ken's book. I know a story and its creator are not the same thing, but you might enjoy knowing that Ken is one of the nicest people I know, while being fiercely intelligent and passionately eloquent about the things he cares about. I love that he is so able to put together strong (perhaps even lawyerly) arguments, but that when you challenge his thinking, he will immediately stop and really think about it. I mean *really* think about it, and possibly chuckle with delight and clap his hands as he pursues new lines of thinking.

Dear friend who has bought the book and is just about to read it. . . I mean why else would you be hanging out in the introduction for this long? I like your style; I'm one of those people that reads introductions too (sometimes when I've finished the book, sometimes before). Virtual high five! We know we're kinda awesome. I hope you will have been going to enjoy the heck out of this book. It made me so happy reading this collection. Some of these stories I'd seen as early drafts, and it's so marvelous to see how Ken is always honing his craft and tuning his stories so that we can't help but be drawn to his characters and fall in love.

This book that you are going to be reading is divided into three sections: *The Law, The Heart,* and *The Law and the Heart*. Within all you will see a reflective tenderness towards humanity, and you will see a light cast towards the processes and structures with which we make sense of the world. Every story engages with two of the central themes of science fiction: How do we construct and make sense of societies? And how do we construct and make sense of ourselves as individuals?

The final story in the collection, "Tenure Track," is one of the first I ever read by Ken and continues to be one of my favorites. Wherever we go in this data-dense world of ours we leave fingerprints, we show preferences, and tell stories in the online groceries we order, the calls to action we respond to, in hospital release forms and donation receipts. Through the simple seeming lens of application forms and seminar registrations, we see a society struggling to deal with the outcomes of extended-life treatments that don't work for everyone. By looking at these fingerprints, we see love, societal upheaval, death, grief, longing and a rebirth. We are future historians, projecting ourselves into implied lives. We empathically extend ourselves into this space and it is a moving experience.

These stories do not provide simple answers, but show wide-ranging adaptive techniques that are seldom perfect as the structures of government, legislation and individuals try to bring their best selves forward in a quickly changing world.

I hope you enjoy this collection as much as I do.

— *Liz Argall, May 7, 2014*

ACKNOWLEDGMENTS

My friend and publisher David Kudler had the idea to assemble this collection in the first place, and has been endlessly patient with my peculiarities along the way. I'm grateful to the editors of the markets in which these stories originally appeared, both for their belief in the work and for their helpful corrections and suggestions: Michele-Lee Barasso, Kaolin Fire, Jessi Hoffman, Kathryn Kulpa, Jonathan Laden, Trevor Quachri, An Owomoyela, Stanley Schmidt, Cat Sparks, and Wendy Dalmeter Theiss, as well as their sundry co-editors and collaborators. Gareth D. Jones, co-author of "Grapple with Thee", graciously consented to its appearance in this collection.

It is astonishing how many people read drafts of these thirteen stories over a period of six years, making crucial comments and suggestions. Primarily these were the members of three critique groups: the Writers' Crucible (Jessica Brockmole, Mary Carroll, Ros Clarke, J. P. Davis, Paula Dooley, Annette Genova); the Clarion Class of 2009 (Heather Albano, Tiffani Angus, Liz Argall, Mishell Baker, Paul Boccaccio, Katie ("Nate") Crumpton, Edward Gauvin, Grady Hendrix, Tanner Jupin, Nina Kuruvilla, Matt London, Val Nolan, Leonard Pung, Shauna Roberts, Eric Schultz, Nicholas Bede Stenner, Nicole Taylor) and our teachers (Holly

Black, Robert Crais, Elizabeth Hand, Larissa Lai, Paul Park, Kim Stanley Robinson, Donald Wesling); and the Cambridge Science Fiction Workshop (Heather Albano, James L. Cambias, F. Brett Cox, Elaine Isaak, Alexander Jablokov, James Patrick Kelly, Steven Popkes, Sarah Smith). Others helped out of pure generosity: Rayna Alsberg, Julie Amberg, Steven Bacher, Sherry Baisden, Guy Bissonnette, Christopher Chien, Meredith Condit Lilea Duran, Marian Gagnon, Gail Kahan, Jeanne Kramer-Smythe, David Kudler, Colleen Less, Dan Less, Ken Liu, Madderbrad, Mary Ann Marcinkiewicz, Ernest Mayo, Thisbe Nissen, Janice Okoomian, Chris Powers, Rachel Schapiro, Carolyn Schneyer, Cinthea Stahl, Geraldine Wagner, David White, and James Boyd White.

Two of these stories were written as part of my 2010 Kickstarter project, "Are You the Agent or the Controller"? Without the backers of that project, they might never have existed.

My father, Jerome J. Schneyer, introduced me to science fiction as soon as I could read, fed my enthusiasm, and praised all my early attempts. He died more than fifteen years before my first story was published, but everything I write grows from that beginning.

And all gratitude ultimately goes to my wife, Janice Okoomian, and our children Phoebe Okoomian and Arek Schneyer, whose patience, forbearance, love and support have been the making of all this work.

Publication History

“Conflagration”: copyright © 2010 by Kenneth Schneyer. This story originally appeared in the *Newport Review* (Summer, 2010).

“I Have Read the Terms of Use”: copyright © 2013 by Kenneth Schneyer. This story originally appeared in *Daily Science Fiction* (December 3, 2013).

“Grapple with Thee”: copyright 2014 by Kenneth Schneyer and Gareth D. Jones. This story appears for the first time in this collection.

“Half a Degree”: copyright © 2014 by Kenneth Schneyer. This story appears for the first time in this collection.

“The Whole Truth Witness”: copyright © 2010 by Kenneth Schneyer. This story originally appeared in *Analog Science Fiction & Fact* (October, 2010).

“Exceptionalism”: copyright © 2014 by Kenneth Schneyer. This story appears for the first time in this collection.

“Life of the Author Plus Seventy”: copyright © 2013 by Kenneth Schneyer. This story originally appeared in *Analog Science Fiction & Fact* (September, 2013).

“Liza’s Home”: copyright © 2009 by Kenneth Schneyer. This story originally published in *GUD: Greatest Uncommon Denominator* (Winter, 2009).

“The Orpheus Fountain”: copyright © 2014 by Kenneth Schneyer. This story appears for the first time in this collection.

“Keeping Tabs”: copyright © 2011 by Kenneth Schneyer. This story originally appeared in *Abyss & Apex* (4th quarter, 2011). It has also appeared on the podcast *Escape Pod* (episode 389, March 28, 2013).

“Hear the Enemy, My Daughter”: copyright © 2013 by Kenneth Schneyer. This story originally appeared in *Strange Horizons* (May 6, 2013).

“The Tortoise Parliament”: copyright © 2010 by Kenneth Schneyer. This story originally appeared in *First Contact: Digital Science Fiction Anthology 1*, edited by Jessi Hoffman (2011).

“Tenure Track”: copyright © 2010 by Kenneth Schneyer. This story originally appeared in *Cosmos Online* (November 23, 2010).

I

The Law

Conflagration

The old man set down the pen and rubbed his wrist. Five letters was a miserable evening's work, but the rheumatism and failing light thwarted him. Only ten years ago, fifteen letters at a sitting would have been an easy chore, even by candlelight. Sometimes Roger imagined that the quenching of his powers was temporary, that tomorrow all would be restored. But such deception never lasted long.

He sealed the letter, pushed his chair away from the writing desk and stood up carefully, feeling fire in every joint. Valetudinarian I've been all my life, discovering a new ailment every week, thought Roger. I might have waited for the real trouble.

The house was mute; he could hear late hoof falls and carriage wheels on Indiana Avenue. Ellen must have gone to bed. Most nights she stayed up until her father retired, but she'd been exhausted this week. It worried him, though it shouldn't. Fatigue in his daughter — fatigue, a chill, an ache in the entrails, in Ellen, Sophie, any of them — tormented Roger with memories of error, disaster and the searing pain of loss.

Again he heard Alice beg to visit her sister in Newport instead of accompanying her parents on holiday. Again he heard his own pig-headed insistence that she oblige him. Again he saw the reports of yellow fever, saw the fear in Alice's eyes, and heard himself reassuring her, reassuring her mother, reassuring all of them — *It is the filth in Norfolk and Portsmouth that lets in the pestilence; here in Old Point Comfort, with good sea air, clean streets and clean rooms, we are protected from it.* Again he saw Anne and Alice collapse, practically in the same moment, wasting away from the fever in barely a day, as if mother and daughter chose to depart together instead of staying with the prideful, guilty father. Careless, careless man. By now Alice might have been married; by now she might even have a child —

He pushed the thought from him, looking up at the portraits of Alice and Anne on the wall. The souls of the faithfully departed need your prayers, not your breastbeating; it is you, Roger Taney, who suffer, and that for a reason. Offer up your burden, and think of the daughters you have.

Not that Ellen stood much risk of a cold in this house. Biting and damp as it was in the street, here it was stifling. A furnace in a dwelling house, who'd have thought of such a thing? He still did not trust it. One day, he thought, it will ignite the whole row, despite what the landlord says. We'll burn to death, like Peter Daniel's poor wife, and there will be an end to my worrying. A fine end — nearly eighty careful years, cosseted and pampered and protecting my health like a newborn babe, to end in sacrificial holocaust, taking my family with me.

Roger grimaced. It was wrong to dwell on such fantasies, or on grief, or on guilt, but it was hard not to be swallowed by thoughts of defeat and black despair. To his friends and colleagues he presented the face of one whose faith sustained him in tragedy, but it was a façade; his heart was being slowly consumed, like a coal in that ominous furnace.

Perhaps things would be different next week, after the decision was announced, after this interminable case was over. It had haunted him for over a year, arriving from the clerk on the very heels of Anne and Alice's deaths. One hearing hadn't been enough, and after two oral arguments he'd seen his Brothers shouting at each other like stevedores across the conference table. In twenty years, this was the first time he'd had to remind them of who they were and what they were doing. It was as if the souls of his wife and daughter, to punish him for his selfishness and pride, had burst the boundaries of Purgatory to torment even the Court, keeping alive this reminder of their agony, visiting a yellow fever of the spirit upon him and those who survived with him. Never to let him rest; he would burn, as their flesh had burned with the fever.

Roger shook his head, coughed, and began to look in the cabinet for a cigar, chiding himself for being ridiculous. God did not permit the souls of the departed to return to earth, and even were He to do so, Anne was the last person who would torment him, no matter how much he deserved it. The case was just a case — a long, complex, politically deadly case, but still a case, one more decision in a string of so many. After it was over, perhaps he could rest for a while.

He found the cigar, cut off the end, and lit it in the candle, watching the flames blossom as he puffed. The smoke in his mouth calmed him as always, and he sat down again.

After a quarter-hour's rumination, he was interrupted by an unfamiliar sound in the hallway beyond the thick door of his study. Something like the hiss of a steam engine and the roar of a bonfire, but with a rapidly descending note like a child's whistle, then followed by a strange echo, as if the sound had been made in a grand rotunda. Roger leaned forward in his chair, listening.

Someone took a step in the hallway. Roger stood up again, cigar in hand.

"Ellen?" But that was not her footstep.

The door of his study opened, and a stranger passed over the threshold.

He was tall, six feet at the least, and clean-shaven, although Taney had never seen side-whiskers quite like these. About thirty-five or forty, with hair clipped short, like a criminal's. His clothes were faintly wrong — Taney couldn't quite place it, but the trousers didn't fall properly, the coat wasn't the right length or even the right weight, and the waistcoat fastened oddly. It was as if this man had just dressed himself for the first time, after seeing others do it, but without quite the knack. He carried the sort of leather bag a lawyer might take to court.

When this interloper entered the room he betrayed surprise, even shock, as if Taney were the last thing he'd expect to find in Taney's own house.

"Mister Chief Justice?" he asked.

Few people addressed Taney in precisely that way, and he was put on his guard immediately.

"Do I know you, sir?"

"No, sir, you don't. My name is Weaver, Henry Weaver." The stranger spoke in an odd, mongrel accent; some of his vowels sounded as if they came from Baltimore, others from Boston, others from the territories.

There was an uncomfortable pause, and Taney cleared his throat. "Mr. Weaver, I hope you will not think me inhospitable, but how do you come to be in my home at this late hour?"

Weaver knitted his brows together and chewed on his lip. "Mister Chief Justice — "

Taney gestured with the cigar. "I think 'Mister Taney' is sufficient for the moment."

"Mr. Taney, explaining how I came to be here is the most difficult thing you could have asked me to do."

Taney tilted his head to one side. "Indeed? How singular. I hope that you have not forced the lock, injured a servant, or entered with the intent to commit a felony?"

"No, sir."

"I am glad to hear it. Well then, if I should not ask you how you came to be here, perhaps you will tell me the purpose of your visit."

A flicker of fear seemed to pass across Weaver's face; then he took a breath and said, "I've come to ask you to reconsider the opinion you are about to issue in the case of *Dred Scott v Sandford*."

Taney felt the heat come to his own face; he took a puff from his cigar to steady himself.

"You are a newspaper reporter," he said.

"No, sir, I'm not."

"Then you have been *reading* the newspapers. How the New York *Herald* obtained what it claims to be the 'opinions' of the Justices is something about which I do not care to speculate, but I assure you that neither you nor Mr. Greeley knows what opinion I am 'about' to issue in the *Scott* case."

"No, sir, I know he doesn't."

"Furthermore, young man, it would be inappropriate in the extreme for me to relate any part of what I plan to decide in a pending case, and it is similarly inappropriate for you to raise the subject."

"Yes, sir, and I apologize. But I know the full text of the opinion you are planning to release."

Taney waved his free hand impatiently. "Nonsense, sir. How could you know it?"

"I've read it."

"But not in the *Herald?*"

"No, sir."

Pointing at Weaver with the cigar, Taney asked, "Then how can you have done so? Has some other broadsheet beaten Mr. Greeley to his prize?"

Weaver opened his bag, pulling out a sheaf of papers, the whitest Taney had ever seen, and surrendered them.

Taney set the cigar in the tray he kept for such purposes and examined the papers. In the center of each leaf was a rectangle of printing Taney recognized immediately, the type and style used by Mr. Benjamin Howard in his reports of Supreme Court cases.

The top of the first page said:

> Report of the decision of the Supreme court of the United States — SUPREME COURT OF THE UNITED STATES. DECEMBER TERM, 1856. DRED SCOTT VERSUS John F. A. Sandford.

Taney turned the first few pages:

> Mr. Chief Justice TANEY delivered the opinion of the court.

And there it was: word for word, comma for comma, the very phrases that Taney had written in longhand, the phrases that were still there if he chose to fetch them. Page after undeniable, relentless page it contained, to the very last sentence. And then — Taney sat down in his chair, waving Weaver to sit as well — all eight of the concurring and dissenting opinions that he had seen only in manuscript drafts, from Wayne's insignificant recapitulation to McLean's broadside attack. Taney felt faint, and the room darkened as if by a sudden rush of smoke. He shut his eyes and put his hand to his heart, waiting for the roaring in his ears to subside. When he opened his eyes again, the page and volume numbers were still visible: volume 19 of Mr. Howard's reports, page 393. No such volume and page had yet appeared, he was sure.

"You — you have had these printed," he said, trying to steady his voice.

"Could I have forged Howard's reports? Would I know the text of your latest revisions?"

"How — " Taney swallowed, and looked up at Weaver. His hands holding the papers shook. "How is this possible?"

Weaver said quietly, "I have come from the future."

"I don't understand you."

"The future, sir. I was born in the year 1997, and before I entered your hallway I was standing in a small, cluttered room in Middletown, Connecticut, on August 23, 2039." He stared Taney in the face, his jaw set.

Taney's throat constricted. He coughed again. "That is absurd."

"I know, sir. But it's the truth."

"It cannot —" A dozen objections rose in Taney's mind, but most of them seemed contradicted by the plain fact of Howard's reports in his hands. He felt faint again.

Then recovered himself; this supposition was irrelevant. "Very well. Let us assume *arguendo* that you are what you claim to be: a man from two centuries hence who has walked into my study." He smiled without humor or pleasure. "May I offer you a cigar?"

"No, thank you, sir."

"You say that you wish me to 'reconsider' the opinion. In what way do you wish it altered? Do you want us to declare, as my Brothers Curtis and McLean would have it, that Dred Scott is a free man?"

Weaver shook his head. "No sir. I know that you couldn't muster a majority for that view. But if you held simply that the matter was a decided issue of Missouri law and not properly before the Court, it would save a lot of trouble. You could avoid ruling on the jurisdictional question, or on the Missouri Compromise, or whether Scott is a slave."

Taney gave him a sour expression, feeling every week of the past year like a stone around his neck. "I have already attempted to do so. Unfortunately, John McLean wants to be President of the United States; he and Benjamin Curtis announced that they would file dissents, covering every issue raised by the litigants, including the constitutionality of slavery. James Wayne and Peter Daniel would not stand for it, and said that they would write replies. The situation became untenable."

Weaver spoke earnestly. "I'll bet that you could convince Wayne and Daniel to join an opinion stating that McLean and Curtis's arguments are beside the point, because the issue is not a matter for the Court."

Taney snorted. "You would make such a wager, would you? With what sorcery shall I persuade them? James Wayne will never stay silent while McLean publishes these sophistries." He smote the pages somewhere near McLean's dissent. "And even if such a thing were practicable, what would be the purpose?"

Weaver looked at the pages in Taney's hands, nodded to himself, then looked up at Taney's face. "Sir, the holdings in this decision, and especially some of the language, will be the most inflammatory document the Court has produced."

Taney narrowed his eyes. "Which language do you mean?"

"The language saying that a negro has no rights a white man is bound to respect." Weaver looked at the ceiling for a moment, then back at Taney. "To many people, that sentence will be the entire holding of the Court."

Again Taney tapped his fingers irritably and painfully on the papers. "The entire holding? It is not a 'holding' of any kind! It is an accurate description of the attitudes of the men who wrote the Constitution."

Weaver leaned forward, as if about to spring from his chair. "It's poison. This decision closes the last door do any sort of compromise on slavery."

"That is not my doing. The Constitution says what it says."

"The Constitution does not say that a black man cannot be a citizen. It does not say that a black man has no rights a white man needs to respect. That is Roger Taney talking."

Taney had spent decades taming his temper; nowadays he merely became flushed when angry. He felt the flush now, like a blaze on his skin. "I resent that, sir. I manumitted my slaves thirty years ago. I pray for the eventual cessation of slavery. But the men who made the Constitution had their own opinions and prejudices, and these are reflected in the document they created."

"Why must they have they intended the document to reflect the worst parts of their natures? Why not assume that they intended the best, instead?"

"And what should I construe their 'best' intent to be? Shall we make the convenient argument that Mr. Sumner and Mr. Beecher are the only true disciples of the Founders, that the Constitution, despite its explicit authorization of slavery, is an Abolitionist declaration?"

"Sir, the Abolitionists will seize upon this decision and turn it into an excuse for confrontation."

Taney looked heavenward. "It is rather late to worry about the actions of the Abolitionists. The suit would not have been filed in the first place, but for the contrivances of the Abolitionists. John Sanford himself is an Abolitionist; so is his brother who arranged the sham sale of Dred Scott, purely to bring this matter before the federal courts! The whole matter is an Abolitionist political device from one end to the other." He raised an eyebrow. "Perhaps you should have *translated* yourself from your Connecticut closet to Mr. Sumner's study back in 1850; then you might have had some effect, if such a man as Sumner can be persuaded by any power on earth."

Weaver straightened in his seat. "Sir, the *Dred Scott* decision will become the rallying cry for Abolitionists and the Republican Party. It will eventually force Senator Douglas into a position on slavery in the territories that will split the Jackson Democrats right down the middle."

Taney looked at him shrewdly. "Governor Seward will become President?"

"No sir."

"Frémont, then? Or Chase?" Taney shuddered at the thought.

"No, sir. Abraham Lincoln of Illinois."

"Lincoln?" The name was not familiar.

"Yes. His election will spur eleven southern states to secede from the Union. Four years of civil war will follow, in which more than half-a-million Americans will die. Finally the Constitution will be amended to outlaw slavery and guarantee the citizenship for the black race. Within a decade, sir, the law will unmake everything the Court's decision in *Dred Scott* says — and it will cost merely an ocean of blood."

Taney's entrails felt as if they had turned to stone. His response came out in a whisper. "Half-a-million dead, years of war, over a *court* decision?"

Unexpectedly, Weaver did not answer at once, but fretted with the cuff of his coat. "Without this decision, maybe the Democratic Party doesn't disintegrate. If people think that compromise is still possible, they may put their faith in Congress to navigate a middle course. Slavery may die a slower death. Secession may happen anyway, but it could be a much smaller rebellion, with fewer states involved. If Virginia doesn't secede, the war won't last long."

Taney hadn't spent nearly sixty years in courtrooms for nothing. "You have used the words *may, maybe, could,* or *might* five times in just a few sentences. You are guessing at all of this, are you not?"

There was another pause before Weaver finally nodded. "No one knows what might have been. But it's my best estimate."

Taney stroked his chin. "I take it that you disapprove of slavery?"

The other looked surprised. "Of course."

"And you say that this, this *civil war* you speak of will end slavery within a decade?"

"Yes."

Taney pursed his lips. "But you believe, you *speculate*, that a future without this war will allow slavery to die a slower death?"

"Yes."

"How slow? Fifty years? A hundred?" Weaver did not answer. Taney pursued, "Have you determined that saving a half-million soldiers, or some portion of a half-million soldiers, is worth leaving *four* million souls and their children in chains for the rest of their lives?"

Weaver looked genuinely perplexed. "Are *you* an Abolitionist?" he asked.

Taney shook his head. "No. But I do not understand how you have come to so prideful and presumptuous a calculation."

Now Weaver's confusion gave way to visible discomfort. A spark kindled in Taney's mind; slowly he said, "I see that I am not the first person to pose this argument to you."

The stranger looked at the floor. "My friends, the others who worked on the displacer, disagreed about the wisdom of trying to change so big an event as the Civil War."

Taney nodded. "You are here without their leave."

Again Weaver did not answer. Taney asked, "What drives you to make so desperate a gamble with so many lives?"

Weaver glared at him furiously, looking like so many cornered advocates Taney had seen. In a different, angry tone, he spat, "I'll tell you one thing, Mr. Taney, one thing that I know *is* certain. The *Dred Scott* decision will wreck the reputation of Roger Brooke Taney forever. A hundred eighty years from now, apart from a few historians and specialists, those who recognize your name at all will know nothing of the war over the Bank of the United States, nor the doctrine of judicial self-restraint, nor anything else you might value. All they will know is that Roger Taney wrote that a black man has no rights a white man is bound to respect. That is your legacy to history — the man who carved racial injustice into the Temple of the American Constitution, until it was blasted away by the indignant fires of God."

At the word "fires," Taney looked up sharply, flicking some cigar ash onto the papers by accident.

"The devil has the power to assume a pleasing shape," he said. "You show me proofs of sorcery, prophesy a fratricidal holocaust in a time when I will surely be dead, and threaten my vanity with tales of what men will say of me in centuries to come. How do I know that you were not sent to tempt me into pride, envy, wrath and despair?"

Weaver stood; Taney followed him creakily, not taking his eyes off the stranger.

"You don't know, sir," Weaver said. "You have only my word for it. But believe me. *Believe me.*" His voice shook. "I've betrayed my friends, risked death, probably ruined my career, to stop a wise man from making the most tragic, stupid decision of his life."

At these words Taney almost interrupted Weaver, for he knew his most stupid, tragic decision was behind him. But the other ploughed on, "So much carnage, and over a document that should never have been written!"

Somewhere behind Weaver's quivering voice and wild eyes there was a story, some other calamity Taney could not make out. A lifetime of cross-examinations told him that Weaver would not answer questions on the subject, no matter how pressed.

The tall man looked at the clock on the shelf. "The displacer is going to call me home in a few minutes. I need those papers, Mr. Taney."

Taney passed the sheaf back to Weaver; the cigar ash fell on the rug. The young apparition put the papers back into his bag and bowed awkwardly from the waist. He said, "Believe me," one more time and stepped out the door.

A moment later, Roger heard the strange, rushing sound of visitation that had heralded Weaver's arrival. He knew that if he followed the messenger's steps into the hallway, he would find nothing.

The cigar was nearly burnt out; the candles were low. Roger looked from side to side, as if Weaver or someone else would appear to trouble him again. Half-a-million dead; had he really the power to stop it with a scratch of the pen? Or to decide instead to perpetuate slavery until its own weight should crush it?

No, Weaver did not know that. Roger had no illusions about his ability to predict the future; he of all people knew the futility of it. The wisest course becomes the deadliest, with no warning.

All Weaver knew was that Roger's name would be reviled, like Benedict Arnold's or Judas Iscariot's. Men would remember him as an author of injustice and inequality. He would be condemned to the flames of history.

Roger looked up at the framed portraits of Anne and Alice. Their steady, blameless gazes reminded him of what he was, what he deserved.

"Let me burn," he rasped. "Let the flames come."

He stubbed out the cigar and snuffed the candle.

Everybody has her favorite "Change the World with Time Travel!" fantasy. After studying Dred Scot v. Sandford *in multiple law school classes, my personal daydream was trying to talk Roger Taney out of rendering that decision, and maybe altering the collision of the Civil War.*

Knowing I wanted to write a story about it, I read Walker Lewis's biography of Taney, learning how the Chief Justice's wife and daughter died of yellow fever shortly before the case was filed, under circumstances where Taney himself arguably bore some blame. This fact overwhelmed everything else; I knew why my time traveler would fail.

I had fun with the fire imagery in this one, and it fit nicely with the facts of Taney's life. He really did think that a furnace in a dwelling house was a crazy and dangerous thing.

— KLS

I Have Read the Terms of Use

As a condition of the use and enjoyment of the Body selected for your use, you agree to the following Terms of Use.

You understand that the aforementioned Body is designed for no more than seventy (70) years of operation, and that attempts to employ said Body for any period beyond the aforementioned duration carries no guarantee that it will function in any capacity. You understand further that We have no control over the actions of other vendors, and that consequently the Body selected for your use may be subject to the actions of other models not within Our control, including infection, infestation, deformation, and decomposition before the expiration of the design period.

You understand further that We have no control over the actions of other Licensees, and that We are not responsible for the uses to which they put the Bodies licensed to them, and that therefore We have no responsibility for murder, rape, mayhem, enslavement, oppression, or heartbreak thereby caused to the Body selected for your use.

You agree not to reverse engineer the Body selected for your use or any of its components or subsystems. You agree that its ultimate design and origins will remain Our proprietary trade secrets, and that you will make no efforts to discover the methods, materials, or first causes We employed in its development. You understand that any efforts on your part to discover, deduce or decode the origins of this Body will lead to false or misleading conclusions concerning Our purposes and plans, and that We have no obligation to correct or otherwise respond to such conclusions.

You understand that the Body selected for your use is a component in a larger system (the "Species") which is itself a component in a larger system (the "Planet") which is itself a component in a larger system (the "Cosmos"). You agree that the function of each component within its system, and its interaction with other components in the system, are Our trade secrets and will not be disclosed to you at any time for any reason. You understand that We will not respond to any inquiries concerning those functions and interactions, and that any attempt by you to determine those functions or interactions will be a breach of these Terms of Use.

You agree that you will be born into a race, class, gender identity, sexuality, state of health, time, and place that will give you no ability to control the circumstances of your own life or effect any change for its improvement, and that whether you are valuable or valueless, skilled or unskilled, ugly or beautiful will depend on the whims of Licensees far away and utterly unknown to you. In the alternative, depending on the availability of various styles, colors, and options, you agree that you will be born into such privilege that you will have no awareness of the customs, preferences, tastes, joys, hopes, fears, or sorrows of any Licensee not nearly identical to yourself, and that, should you obtain information pertaining to your own acquiescence, responsibility, or culpability for, without limitations, the deprivations, pains, illnesses, dismemberment, torture, rape, or murder of Licensees not nearly identical to yourself, you will treat such information as Our intellectual property and none of your business, and will, to the extent practicable, understand such matters to be no fault of yours, and contrary to your own good intentions.

You understand that the Body selected for your use is provided with a number of factory settings concerning the cultural norms under which it will operate (the "Starting Conditions"). You understand further that the Starting Conditions will be predetermined by existing relationships of power and wealth within the Culture of which said Body is a component. You agree that the Starting Conditions will determine your perceptions of morality and ethics, and that those perceptions will regard the existing power and wealth relationships of said Culture to be appropriate, functional and beneficial.

You agree that you will not use the Body selected for your use to infringe upon, alter, or amend any of the Starting Conditions, and that the distribution of goods, services, nutrition, medicine, affection, sexual gratification and emotional support shall be substantially similar when you surrender the Body selected for your use as when said Body was initially provided.

You agree to experience persistent confusion and disorientation concerning right action, wrong action, your obligations to your family, friends, community, nation, the Species, the Planet, and the Cosmos, resulting in paralysis and inactivity concerning any matter of ethical or moral significance. In the alternative, depending on market conditions and supplies, you agree to experience irrational certainties and extreme passions concerning such matters, in which case you have sole responsibility for any resultant damage.

You understand that We disclaim any representations or warranties other than those contained in these Terms of Use, and that no oral, psychological, historical, literary, or religious assurances you may have received from persons purporting to be Our agents will be binding on Us. You understand further that We expressly disclaim any implied warranties, including, without limitation, any implied warranty of survivability, likability, employability, health, sanity, or fitness for a particular purpose. You agree to hold Us harmless from any direct, consequential, or incidental damages that may result from noncompliance with any assurances or implied warranties not contained in these Terms of Use.

You agree that these Terms of Use shall be subject to such natural, moral, and spiritual laws as We have previously enacted, and that it is your responsibility to acquaint yourself with such laws. You agree that disputes concerning these Terms of Use shall be resolved by adjudicators of Our choosing, in a time and manner that seems best to Us.

You agree that We may alter these Terms of Use on one generation's notice to you. You may refuse such alterations by surrendering the Body selected for your use, at such time and place as We shall designate.

Any use of this Body, including but not limited to breathing, eating, drinking, sleeping, working, playing, loving, or hating, shall be deemed acceptance of these Terms of Use, and shall be irrevocably binding upon you and your heirs, devisees, grantees and assigns forever.

I've read too many contracts in my time, and have long hated lengthy, one-sided "agreements" that no one intends to negotiate in good faith, and which offer the other party any real choice. I also brood about the fact that so much of our lives is dictated by our circumstances, that what we perceive as naturally "right," "reasonable," and "fair" is nothing more than a reflection of the relative power with which we were born. And of course, in the Western religions, God has made covenants with some or all people, promising to do things in exchange for their faith and obedience.

These three things together made me imagine God's covenant as User License Agreement, replete with our acquiescence to all the horrible things we suffer and do to each other, to our own ignorance, to our own futility. Of course it's satire, but of course it hurts.

— KLS

Grapple with Thee

by Kenneth Schneyer & Gareth D. Jones

Letter fragment, handwritten by Stanley Temple:

> ...seen what they do, and still you trivialize them. Every grab for power begins with small movements by someone who seems too eccentric to be noticed.
>
> You'll say this isn't politics, it's business. But it's business about *communication*, and communication is where democracy comes from! Why should it surprise you that I dedicate myself to opposing them to my last gasp? Rather than calling me names and trying to talk me out of it, you...

Violet loves her wall, where Mommy painted Mushroom the Dog. In springtime she watched as Mommy made the pencil outline, looking at Mushroom on the cover of Violet's pink-and-purple *Animal Friends* book. Mushroom is always on the cover of the books, because he's the best one. Violet saw Mommy mix the colors on her little board — she called it a "pal." She said she had her pal when she was younger, when she did lots of painting; she misses painting, and that's why she was so happy to paint Mushroom on the wall for Violet.

Now Mushroom the Dog stands at the foot of Violet's bed, where she can see him when she goes to sleep and wakes up. She has her own toy Mushroom too, and she puts him at the foot of the bed, so that she can look at both of them at once. Sometimes she pretends they're Mommy Mushroom and Baby Mushroom, and she makes up stories about them. Andy said that Mushroom is a boy, and that boys can't be mommies, but he's always saying stupid things like that.

Everybody loves Mushroom on the wall (except Andy). Thayla was over last week, and took a picture with her Pinkie Dear camera. She told Violet that her own daddy liked it so much that he put the picture up on the memory link.

Today Violet, Mommy, Mommy Mushroom and Baby Mushroom are having tea on Violet's bed. She's made cookies for her and Mommy, and dog food cookies for the two Mushrooms.

"That," says Mommy, "is the best tea I ever tasted. However do you do it, Miss Violet?"

"Well," says Violet, "It's a secret."

Mommy nods. "I know; the best artists always have their secrets, don't they? We don't let anyone know how we do it."

"That's right," says Violet. "Especially the dog food."

"Especially the dog food," agrees Mommy.

There's a knock at the door of Violet's room.

"Come in," she says. "This is our tea party."

The door opens and it's Daddy, wearing his work clothes and holding a letter. The letter has a purple heart with a pink star on it, just like Violet's book. "Good afternoon, Violeta Violin. Hi, sweetie."

Mommy's eyebrows go up. "Roger! You're early. What's the occasion?"

"I got some mail that I thought you'd want to see. It's from Lewit."

"Lewit?"

Violet knows that name. "Lewit? Is he the one who makes the Lewitfics? Can I talk to him?"

"Maybe later, Vio. Actually —" Daddy looks straight at Mommy, not at Violet. "It's from Lewit's lawyers."

♎

Letter from Richard C. Greening, Attorney at Law, to Roger Walloon, 20 November 2069:

> Dear Mr. Walloon:
>
> I represent the Sandy Lewit Corporation, owner of the copyrights and trademarks associated with the fiction, cartoon, vid and Lewitfic® character Mushroom the Dog®.
>
> It has come to our attention that you have, without the permission of Lewit, reproduced the image of Mushroom the Dog, specifically the image appearing on the cover of *Lewit's Most Beloved Animal Friends*™, as a mural on an interior wall of your premises, permitting that image to be uploaded onto a publicly-accessible memory account. Reproduction of a copyrighted image without the permission of the owner is a violation of federal laws. Injunctive remedies, statutory damages and even criminal sanctions may result.
>
> We demand that you immediately remove the image from your premises. Failure to comply will result in our seeking appropriate legal remedies.
>
> Should you wish to contact me regarding this matter, I can be reached at the phone number and email address above.
>
> Respectfully,
>
> Richard C. Greening

Greening fidgets in his chair, stands up, walks across the office to the doorway, looks out, walks back to his chair, sits down again. He puts his palms together in a simulated gesture of composure. *Get a grip on yourself*, he thinks. *He's not due for five more minutes.*

But how could he not be excited? A job in Lewit's IP division right out of law school, assignments for "Investigation, Warning and Negotiation" within the first month — and now he's going to have an actual negotiation! Until this week, his letters received meek, compliant answers or meeker silence. It's gratifying to be so effective, and Blau is delighted with his work, but Greening is itching to test himself against another lawyer, somebody who fights back.

Consequently, when Walloon's lawyer sent the e-mail saying he'd drop in to discuss the matter, Greening was thrilled. The senior attorneys have been coaching him: don't make concessions, probe for information, remember that you're the one in the favorable position. You'd think he'd never studied negotiation techniques! And since none of them has seen any of the relevant documents, this is generic advice they'd give to anyone. The man's network profile is one of the most utilitarian Greening has seen: a brief synopsis of his legal qualifications and career, the only personal note being that he likes classical music. It doesn't specify listening or playing.

His monitor flashes and Eddie's voice comes over the speakers. "Mr. Greening, Stanley Temple is here to see you."

Greening clears his throat. "Send him in, Eddie." His voice comes out higher than usual.

As Temple enters the office, Greening's first impression is of the color grey. Temple is a tall, bony man of about forty whose slightly too-long, light brown hair has an outer film of grey, as if someone has sprayed frost on his head without bothering to comb it in. His skin too, stretched over the bones of his face, has a faint greyness, although that might be beard; he seems not to have shaved carefully this morning. Hanging on his body is a once-expensive, light grey suit that has been worn for years without replacement or repair; there are frays on the cuff, and a seam is beginning to separate on the shoulder. One of the buttons on the jacket has been replaced; a spot on the trousers betrays a sheen. His shoes would be black if they had been polished recently, but the heels and toes are both worn to a dull grey. Greening's own shoes are so new that they squeak, and he removed the thread at the vent of his jacket only when Blau pointed it out to him two weeks ago.

"Richard Greening?" Temple asks as Greening stands. His voice is quiet and low in pitch, but it sounds as if he's squeezing his diaphragm to get out every word, as if he's restraining some powerful impulse or feeling. His eyes, also grey, are fever-bright.

Temple's hand, chapped and ice cold, seems to suck the warmth and moisture from Greening's sweaty palms. In the handshake, too, there is some repressed effort, as if Temple is exercising all his will to keep himself from crushing Greening's hand.

Greening gestures for Temple to sit. On his way down, the man's eyes light on the toy at the corner of Greening's credenza. "I see you have Mushroom the Dog."

"Yes. Central office is always sending reproductions and samples to the employees, to spread the brand around, you know. Would you like it?"

Temple nods slowly, not taking his eyes off the toy. "Yes, I would."

Greening feels that he's already betrayed a weakness, giving away Lewit property to an adversary. Nonetheless he reaches behind him with his right arm, snags the tiny Mushroom between two fingers and hands it to Temple, who carefully puts it in the inside pocket of his jacket.

Temple settles back in his chair, although his posture remains tense. "Why don't you re-state your position, Mr. Greening?"

"Briefly, we would like the infringing image removed from Mr. Walloon's property."

"That's very succinct. Are you willing to defray the cost of the alteration?"

"Certainly not. Why should we pay to abate harm that your client has caused us?"

"Why indeed?" sighs Temple. He pauses for a moment, and continues in a sad tone. "Tell me, Greening, do you often send threatening letters to four-year-old girls?"

Greening sits straighter. "I resent that. I sent a letter to Roger Walloon."

"It's going to amount to the same thing." Temple gives him what might be a pitying smile. "You're a shark, Greening. You prey on the weak and defenseless. But you're not inescapable."

When Greening doesn't answer, Temple continues, "Shall I tell you what I think is going to happen?"

"If you like."

"I think that, within the next 48 hours, you are going to write to me, on Lewit letterhead, saying that you retract your earlier statements and that Lewit Corporation has no intention of making any claims as to the mural on Violet Walloon's bedroom wall. You'll say you acknowledge the wall to be Roger Walloon's property, the artwork to be Katya Walloon's property, and you might even be cute and acknowledge the *room* to be Violet Walloon's property. It would also be nice if you threw in a comment that Lewit is delighted that an artist like Katya Walloon gave such a tribute to the character of Mushroom the Dog, because it will add to the popularity of your brand." Temple is smiling now.

Greening guffaws. "Oh, really? And why on earth would I do that?"

Temple gazes at the ceiling, considering the question. Like the ceiling of every office in the building, this one is decorated with the Lewit trademark, a pink star superimposed over a purple heart. "Well, first of all, this is the weakest infringement claim I have seen in fifteen years. The mural fits squarely within at least two black-letter exceptions I can cite without cracking a book; it's the sort of case that gets knocked out on summary judgment, maybe on the pleadings. Since no court is going to believe that a copyright attorney didn't *know* of those exceptions, the letter may constitute harassment and/or a deliberate attempt to mislead a layman about the law; it's probably my duty to report you to the Disciplinary Board."

Greening's gut squeezes; he swallows hard. Then he takes a deep breath and replies, "Perhaps, but we can let a court decide that."

"As you wish. We'll find out soon, because in 48 hours I'm filing an action against Lewit for a declaratory judgment that there is no infringement of any kind. Within 24 hours after service of process I'll be noticing the deposition of Eugene Hammersmith."

"Hammersmith?" Greening's mouth is dry. "Are — are your clients really willing to pay for all this, rather than just cleaning up a mural?"

Temple tut-tuts. "Shame on you, Mr. Greening. You shouldn't be asking about conversations between a lawyer and his client. However, I don't think my clients will mind my telling you that this isn't going to cost them anything; I'm doing the whole case *pro bono*, including the discovery costs."

Greening's jaw drops. "But why?"

Again Temple studies the purple heart above him. "That's my business. Feel free to speculate. Perhaps I feel sorry for Violet Walloon, who's scared she's going to lose her beloved Mushroom. Perhaps I feel like doing a good deed. Perhaps I hate you." His tone hasn't changed; he's still looking at the heart.

"There's more," Temple continues. "Contemporaneously with the filing of this action I'll publish a press release. I think *Lewit Sues Little Girl for Bedroom Wall* is a catchy headline, don't you? I can't imagine there's an editor in North America who wouldn't love to use it. Actually I should thank you, Greening; I'll be invited to speak on *Events Now*, on *Tommy Dalton*, on *Mornings with Marney*. I'll be famous: Stanley Temple, Champion of Children Against Big, Mean Multis. The new clients alone will more than pay my fee for this case."

Greening has the feeling that Temple neither wants to be famous nor cares about new clients.

"Oh, and then there's the merchandising. We'll print up tee-shirts with the slogan, *Lewit Bullies Kids*. I'm sure we'll sell 100,000 within two weeks."

"That's libel!"

"Matters of opinion aren't defamatory, and truth is an absolute defense."

"You'll never be able to prove *truth*."

"Oh, we won't send shirts to jurisdictions that follow the English Rule. The bottom line is that my clients are going to make a large profit out of this dispute, but it's going to cost Lewit millions in lost revenue and goodwill. Or you can write me that letter I mentioned."

Greening stammers for a moment, then gets a grip on himself. "This is absurd!"

"*Absurd* is exactly the right word. If you had consulted the marketing or public relations arms of Lewit before writing that *absurd*, juvenile document, it never would have been sent. But you know, there is an alternative."

Temple leans across the desk, getting his face as close as he can to Greening's without getting up, lowering his voice conspiratorially. "The two of us could step outside and settle this matter like gentlemen. Actually I'd prefer it that way." He grins broadly, showing all his teeth, and Greening has the irrational idea that Temple wants to take a bite out of his face. He flinches.

"Th-that's completely uncalled for," Greening says.

"Completely," agrees Temple, still leaning over the desk.

"If you engage in physical threats, I'll have to have you removed from the building!"

"Oh, that won't be necessary." Temple rises slowly to his feet, looking down at Greening. "Forty-eight hours, Mr. Greening. After that it's newsblogs, declaratory judgments and tee-shirts."

"I can't possibly get approval for such a letter in 48 hours," says Greening.

"Oh, I'm certain you can. And if you're lucky, they won't fire you for writing the first letter." With that, Temple turns and vanishes through the doorway, humming something orchestral as he goes.

♎

After her meeting with the congresswoman, Alba practically skips down South Main Street in search of coffee. On the vid screens, kiosks, and sides of the buses, she sees ads for the latest vid, Lewit's *Blue Avenger*, for the new update on animation software bearing the heart-and-star logo, and for six new titles of Lewitfics. She doesn't notice the grey suit that sidles up next to her.

"If it isn't the Political Consultant to the Stars," says the all-too-familiar voice.

Without looking at him, she says, "If it isn't the Lawyer to the Masses. Hello, Stan."

"Hi, Alba."

She looks over her right shoulder. Stanley is as imposing as ever, but he seems thinner, paler and more nervous; he hasn't shaved well, and that's not like him. How long has it been? More than a year, anyway, possibly two...

Who am I kidding? It's been fourteen-and-a-half months.

Aloud she says, "How are you? How's the crusade?"

"The same," he says, smiling a little. "And you? How's getting people into office?"

"Actually I just got a new gig. Pheobe Boncoeur."

"The Senate race?"

Alba grins broadly.

"Well done indeed, Alba." Then his face lights up with comprehension. "Ah, so *that's* what you're doing on South Main! You were just in her office."

"Yes, and now I'm searching for coffee to celebrate. I was heading for Sbux."

"*Sbux?*" Stanley's face is revolted. "That's not a celebration, it's a penance. I can give you proper coffee. The apartment's only —"

"I remember where the apartment is, Stanley. I don't want to trouble you."

"No trouble at all."

Her better judgment says *No*, but Stanley has such a lonely look about him. "All right," she says "But Stan? In the word 'ex-wife,' the emphasis is on the first syllable."

He nods quickly, not quite hiding the wince. "Of course, honey. I know that."

Stanley lives above his office. It's not where *they* lived, but afterwards he moved to be closer to his work. You couldn't get much closer than this; the Supreme Court building is maybe fifteen minutes' walk away, the Federal building twenty-five, as are the banks. The vid studio outposts, media outlets and tech firms that are his clients or opponents are a twenty-minute climb up the Hill. If a man wanted to do nothing but represent and sue people, he'd be in the ideal location.

No, that's not fair. There other things nearby too: art galleries, splendid restaurants, the only two non-Lewit bookstores within a mile, some very pleasant clubs — but she doubts that Stanley frequents them. His work consumes his life, his only relaxation is his personal music collection.

Alba follows Stanley through the door at the top of the stairs. She's been here before once or twice, but now the room seems much more dimly lit. Then she sees the photographs. Three of the walls of the room are covered with portrait photos in dark frames, absorbing the brightness cast by the overhead light. Alba's been in many a politician's office, and she's used to self-important frescoes of autographed shots showing the occupant with various Great Men. Stanley's walls resemble those, except that these photos are in identical frames, in neat rows and columns; it reminds her of a cemetery.

Stanley has gone into the kitchen, beyond the half-wall, where the wall is bare save for a small painting of a stylized whale. There, on the small work surface, sits his pride and joy, the best coffee press money can buy. Typical of Stanley: in a dwelling where other objects are shabby, secondhand or missing, the coffee apparatus would fit in well with copper pans and caviar. The beans are custom-imported and roasted by Stanley himself; he spoons some into a mortar and begins to pound them while he waits for the spring water to heat. When he's pulverized the beans satisfactorily he tips them into the press, then turns off the kettle as the water begins to boil and sticks a thermometer into it. He'll wait until the temperature dips below 190°F before he pours the water over the grounds. Then he'll wait exactly five minutes before pressing down the screen, which he won't allow to descend all the way. Alba pushes away the thought that she misses the ritual.

Stanley pours two cups. His will be black, of course; nothing should interfere with the perfect bean. In hers he puts the sugar and cream in exactly the proportions she likes; he has fresh cream in his refrigerator although he never uses it himself. She follows the cups to the table, where a neat stack of last century's legal volumes form the only clutter.

Alba sighs into her cup. "You still make the best cup of coffee in North America, Stan."

"I told you: a celebration requires the proper ingredients." He lifts his cup in a toast, then says, "Now tell me all about Phoebe Boncoeur."

She tells him why Phoebe is the best candidate she's worked for in years, how this will open doors for her, the strategies she plans to use — all while he sits with his chin on his palm, an indulgent smile on his face. He listens so well.

But as she speaks, she cannot escape the faces on the wall. They seem to be listening too, and they are less approving, less supportive. Their expressions don't change and they don't nod; they stare. Gradually she runs down.

"Stanley," she asks, feeling that it's going to be a mistake but unable to stop. "Who's in those pictures?"

"Ah." He pushes his coffee cup away from him, not towards her but as far across the table as his hands will reach. Then he stands and walks over to the wall like a docent in a museum. In the weirdly muffled light, he looks like he's surrounded by a pale blue halo. He points to one photograph, a smiling young man in a sweater.

"This is Julian Khasraji. Julian used to be a documentary filmmaker. Several years ago, Lewit Corporation notified all of Julian's distributors that his films contained fleeting images of billboards, snippets of songs, or some words of texts that were owned by Lewit, for which he had not sought permission. They indicated that, if the distributors trafficked in any of Julian's films, they would lose access to any Lewit productions. Julian wasn't able to get a single film shown after that. Now he works as a cashier in a convenience store; I think he's on antidepressants."

Stanley gestures at a photo of a middle-aged woman with striking cheekbones. "And this is Miranda O'Connell. Miranda was once a songwriter, but her contract with Sonic Boom Productions — a Lewit subsidiary — stipulated that she lost essentially all control over her music, in exchange for what barely amounted to a living wage. She quit and tried to find another label, but she'd been blackballed. I have no idea where she is, but she isn't making music."

His face has begun to color. Another photo. "Oscar Gianninni. Worked for Lewit as a software designer, but wrote fiction on the side. He completed his novel, and Lewit claimed that it was a work-for-hire, that they owned the whole thing, every scrap. It was nonsense, but they threatened to sue and he didn't have the money to defend himself. Lewit published the book and it became a best seller; I think the vid rights netted them more than twenty million. Oscar took an overdose three years ago."

Stanley is breathing hard. Alba's eyes are wide and her cup shakes.

"He wasn't a client?" she asks.

"No. Only a few of them were clients. Not nearly enough. They all *lost*, though; they've all been outflanked, outmuscled, crushed, obliterated. Lewit Almighty, Lewit of a Thousand Faces, Lewit the All-Destroying. You'd be surprised how many of them are dead." His eyes are blazing.

Alba rises. "Oh, Stanley. And they're all on your wall?"

"Someone has to honor them. Someone has to remember them. Someone has to avenge them."

"You can't keep doing this."

"I *have* to keep doing this," he barks. He lowers his eyes, rubs his forehead. "You know, I always thought of them as a shark, but they're not." He gestures across at the kitchen wall. "Lewit is more like a whale, opening its mouth, swallowing everything in its path." He looks up defiantly. "But I won't let them continue conquering."

Again she can't help herself, though she knows that it won't do any good. "But you're pushing against a mountain, Stan! You're trying to order back the tide! All they're doing is protecting their property —"

It's the wrong thing to say. Stanley advances on her quickly, snarling into her face, "It isn't about *property*. It was never about *property*."

She's trembling all over. It's always going to end the same way. She flees down the stairs, running out the door and not stopping for two blocks.

She leans against the rough brick of a building she doesn't recognize, trying to catch her breath, trying not to cry. On her way out of the apartment she glimpsed one of the walls of Stanley's shrine, his macabre gallery of the victims of Lewit.

Stanley's own portrait was among them.

Internal e-mail, Quantum Change Software LLC:

From: Natalie Ridolfski
To: Bill Yee
Date: 25 March 2051
Subj: Stanley & ReinventWare
Hi Bill,

I've summarized the Stanley situation below, as discussed earlier.

When I told Stanley the patent application had been granted, I'd never seen him look happier. He didn't stop speaking for five minutes, said his mother would be happy to have a "known inventor" for a son; he was going to call his girlfriend right away, wanted to have the patent framed, ReinventWare was the most exciting creative experience of his life, he felt a real sense of accomplishment, he was enthusiastic about working on the GroundZero project, etc etc.

When I told him we'd sold the patent to Lewit, and how big the price was, he looked shocked and disappointed. He said something like, "So this means it's theirs, not mine?" I told him his name is still on the patent as "Inventor", the only difference is that Lewit, rather than Quantum, would be listed as "Owner." All he said was, "But why did you sell it?"

I reminded him that Quantum is in the software *design* business, and we don't do marketing or implementation. He just kept saying, "Why *them*?" I don't know what he has against them. He knows they're the buyer-of-choice for nearly every new title that comes out.

Then he asked about the money. "So out of all these millions of dollars, how many will I see?" He must know already, he created ReinventWare as a work-for-hire, his reward is his salary (which must be pretty good). He wanted to know about residuals and royalties, which he won't get.

He was pretty upset that Lewit won't want him to continue to work on ReinventWare.

You know that expression, "His face fell"? I could literally see Stanley's face falling during the conversation, and when I told him that he'd no longer have any role with the project, it was like someone undid the catch on a Venetian blind: Wham!

I tried to cheer him up by reminding him how exciting the GroundZero project was going to be. He looked at me like I'd just killed his puppy, and said, "What's the point?"

I haven't been able to get more than three consecutive syllables out of Stanley since then. I don't know how this is going to pan out, but something about the Lewit thing has taken all the wind out his sails. We might need to start looking for someone to fill his shoes; he may not be with us much longer.

♎

It is a lovely day for a protest march. Sherman's happy to be outdoors, although he'd prefer to be lolling on a green lawn with a dark-eyed, soft-skinned companion, rather than retracing the same thirty-two paces in front of this massive wall emblazoned with a giant heart and star. Still, it's a good cause. His paces are accompanied by stirring fanfares from the speaker set on Temple's picket board. It's something very old, probably out of copyright, certainly pre-Lewit.

Temple strides up beside him, shouting slogans until his voice is hoarse. *He* certainly doesn't have any regrets about not lolling on a lawn; Temple would probably think it was a distraction from the urgent task of bringing down a corrupt media empire.

"Bring up the pace, Gelb!" he urges Sherman. Temple's sign says *35% of All Writers Is Too Many*! Sherman's own sign says *Who Controls 65% of Video Productions*? Tina is carrying the slogan *75% Share of Software? Ridiculous*! Sherman, Tina and others argued that these signs were too factual, not emotional enough. But when they suggested trying more evocative slogans, Temple came up with things like *Burn This Building To the Ground*! and *String 'Em Up*! Imagining what the police would do with that, the others relented and went back to toting statistics.

The crowd in front is so small that Sherman can't tell whether they're watching the march or just stopping to catch their breath on the way to the bus. There is one newsblog reporter and one vidcatcher covering the march, but they're not major names. *All in all*, Sherman Gelb thinks as he considers the blister forming on his right heel, *it would have been better to go to the park.*

Thankfully it's not too long until their allotted hour runs out. Temple shakes the hand of everyone who volunteered and promises to let them know when the next march is planned. Sherman walks back across town with Temple, helping him carry the signs. Aside from discussing the march, Sherman has little idea what else to talk about with Temple.

"You want to stop at the bar for a drink?" he asks. Might be a way to break the ice, and Sherman certainly needs something to sooth his parched throat.

Temple flinches, gives him an odd look, almost offended, somehow haunted. "No. Thanks."

Sherman shrugs and they walk in silence for a moment.

"I thought that went very well," Temple says eventually.

"Not many people, though. Not a lot of coverage," ventures Sherman.

"No matter, no matter. It's all a question of building momentum."

If this is momentum, thinks Sherman, *we're going to have all the impact of a large bag of feathers*. Aloud, he says, "I don't see how a series of marches is going to do that."

"It's marches and other things," says Temple.

"Oh?"

"Yes; I know Lewit won't change its business model just because of some lawsuits and protesters in front of the Providence branch office." As usual, it's the one topic that will get Temple talking.

"So what are you talking about?"

"Well," says Temple, lowering his voice and glancing around him. "I've been communicating with the senior executives about their past."

"Their past."

"Yes; also their present."

There is a pause. "And?" prompts Sherman.

"Oh, let's just say that there are some events and practices, some of a business nature and some not, which I imagine Hammersmith wouldn't be delighted to have published. I think it would give the whole world a different view of what sort of person he is. Actually I think it'd give his *wife* a whole different view."

"You're blackmailing Eugene Hammersmith?" Now Sherman wants to look around for listeners too.

"I did not say that. And Hammersmith isn't the only one with whom I've been communicating."

"My god."

"Yes, it turns out that there are exotic bits of recent history concerning Xavier, Longfellow, Glynn, even Fishkill. The most astonishing things."

"Stanley, these 'exotic facts' — they weren't just lying around, waiting to be found."

"Not exactly. But I have a knack for designing investigative algorithms. It used to be my profession, actually, before..." He pauses, starts afresh. "There are certain mathematical relationships between disparate facts that can, if iterated a sufficient number of times, yield high probabilities of truth."

"High probabilities? High probabilities aren't going to result in a court case."

"They don't need to, not if they're right."

"Because of your private communications with the persons involved."

"Just so. Use the right bait, even the biggest fish can be caught."

Sherman has the feeling that seventeen vid cameras, eight microphones and a few rifles are pointing at him. He tries to speak without moving his mouth. "The CEO, the CFO, the CLO, a Division President and the General Counsel. May I ask — I don't think I want to ask, actually."

"Probably wise. But I'm hopeful that I can gain certain concessions."

"You're not asking for money, are you?"

"*Money*? From *Lewit*? I thought you knew me better than that." Temple looks hurt. "No. I'm just hoping for certain concessions to be made in matters related to the enforcement of their so-called property rights."

Sherman takes Temple by the shoulder and speaks in a near-whisper. "You are playing with fire, you lunatic. Those guys are not going to sit still and let you do this."

Temple considers the idea. "People have said that before about my various actions against Lewit, but usually they've been wrong."

"But this is different."

"Just in degree, not in kind. It's just a way of making them see how to do the right thing."

Sherman is trying to find a way of saying that this is possibly the craziest statement he has ever heard, even from Temple, when they reach the door of Temple's office. Temple takes the signs from Sherman, shakes his hand, thanks him for his help, and closes the door in his face.

Patient history on Isaac Temple, taken by Jerome Snow, M.D.:

Chief Complaint: Alcohol addiction.

History of Present Illness: Habitual drinking began eight years ago, when patient lost his job at Tamarind Music Systems upon takeover by Lewit Corp. Patient had trouble obtaining other work, although he eventually found something in another field. Apparently the period of unemployment and dissatisfaction with the new job was the trigger for the initial drinking habit. Patient was urged to seek treatment by his wife; she threatened to leave him if he continues drinking. Behavior while intoxicated oscillates between depressed paralysis and rage.

Personal Medical History: Patient is 48-year-old male, married (wife: Esther, 46) with one child (son: Stanley, 13). Patient has not had a regular physical examination for at least ten years. No serious complaints before drinking began.

Family History: No family history of alcoholism or other addiction disorder. Father (77) is mildly depressive; mother died at 64, stroke.

Review of Symptoms: Patient admits to loss of appetite, frequent thirst and nausea. Visually observed yellow tinge to skin and eyes, swelling at the midsection and several unhealed bruises. Patient was mildly febrile upon intake; examination revealed abdominal tenderness.

> *Diagnosis/Recommendations*: Given symptoms of (possibly advanced) liver disease, referred patient to Hepatology Clinic at RWMC.
>
> *Prognosis*: Unclear whether patient will survive long enough to benefit from addiction treatment.

Alba's phone wakes her in the middle of the night.

"What?" her voice sounds hollow.

"Alba." Stanley's voice.

"Stanley? What time is it?"

"Uh, three-thirty."

"*Three-thirty*? Stanley, what is it? Did something happen? Is everyone all right?"

"Sorry, Alba. I was working on something and I didn't realize how late it was." He sounds wired, like he's had a dozen cups of coffee, like he's just won a case, like he's about to pull her clothes off. Like that ever happened.

"I can only imagine what you were working on," she moans. *This is why, this is why.*

"Yeah, well, listen. Since you're up anyway —"

"Since I'm *up anyway*? Lucky for you it's Saturday. I don't have to be up early."

"Just listen!" He could be dancing at the other end of the phone. "Lewit and the other big multis have all the protection of the law behind them, right? They get copyright changed, or antitrust changed, to suit them just as they like."

"Yeah. So?" *Nothing* ever changes.

"But that's just because the politicians need them and can use them, isn't it? I mean, if a multi became a real political liability, the politocos would dump it in a minute, wouldn't they? Leave it to twist in the wind?"

"What do you mean, 'political liability?'" She sits, pulls the sheet up around herself.

"Well, you remember Bergerian? After the fraud was discovered? All of those senators behind the coal protection bills just abandoned them, right?"

"Sure they did. They still get elected by their constituents, and no money from Bergerian was going to help them if the voters got angry. Some of them lost the next election anyway."

"That's it, that's the *point*. And if Lewit were caught in something big, it could lose all of its protection too!"

Alba snorts and falls back onto the pillow, still holding the phone. "It'd have to be *really* big. So many of them are huge Lewit supporters." She yawns, scratching her leg.

"What if Lewit had planned a murder?"

"What?" She sits bolt upright. "Murder?"

"Yeah. What if the officers of Lewit had planned a murder to further company policy?"

"Stanley, what's going on? What are you mixed up in?"

"C'mon, just play along. What if they'd planned a murder?"

She counts to five and closes her eyes. "All right. Planning a murder would be pretty bad, yes. They'd lose a lot of support in the Senate, more in the House. But you know, inchoate crimes like attempt, conspiracy, they all look fishy to the average person. People wonder whether it's all a sham. It could be spun to look like a setup by Lewit's political enemies, such as, for example, you."

"Yeah, but what if the murder were really carried out? What if it were 100% proven?"

"That'd be poison. Nobody would touch them. They might find themselves victims of all sorts of enforcement actions."

"Yes."

"But Stan, this is just a matter of probability. Who knows the cattle-prods or inducements Lewit's acquired over the years? It might be that even something as bad as that wouldn't be the coffin nail."

"But this is still the best chance." His voice is suddenly a lot calmer. "It's the harpoon I've been looking for."

"But Stanley, what are you — *Stanley*!"

The line has gone dead.

Electronic message recovered from the memory account of Stanley Temple, pursuant to Providence Police Investigation 2070-783:

From: [Name and tracking masked]
To: Stanley Temple
Date: 5 August 2070 23:54
Subj: Warning

The thread below is genuine. I'm no friend of yours, but this sort of thing is wrong. Take precautions.

From: Pest Control
To: Central
Date: 3 August 2070 01:47
Subj: Re: Remediation

Understood. Remediation will occur on August 9.

From: Central
To: Pest Control
Date: 3 August 2070 01:35
Subj: Remediation
Per our earlier conversation, temple infestation should be remedied expeditiously. Infestation reliably appears Saturday 6:45 PM #60; pest can be isolated first Warren stop.

Investigator's Notes: Internal evidence shows that Temple, during the period 5-8 August 2070, used previously unknown tracing software to identify "Central" as Eugene Hammersmith, CEO of the Sandy Lewit Corporation, and "Pest Control" as Martha Lopak, a known felon arrested, but never indicted, for three homicides on the eastern seaboard between 2062 and 2069. Temple left the file, with all tracing data, in a prominent location in the memory account, linked to other files showing that Hammersmith and other officers of Lewit had engaged in certain illegal activities, including attempts to circumvent securities and antitrust laws. The files were identified with the tag, "Early Labor Day Gift."

♎

Rosie wishes the bus would come. It seems like forever, and she's hot and so excited that she can't wait. But Mama will get mad if Rosie asks her, yet again, when the bus is coming. She's biting her lip and trying not to say it when she notices the man.

Rosie's never seen a man like this before, with hair that's both tan and grey. He's wearing a grey suit that's just the color of his hair, and despite the heat isn't sweating; people who are hot sweat. Perspire, Mama says.

The man sees Rosie and smiles at her. His smile is strange, sort of happy and sad at the same time. If Mama weren't there, Rosie thinks she'd be afraid. But Mama squeezes Rosie's hand reassuringly and she knows it's all right.

"You're all dressed up," Rosie says to the man.

"So are you," he says, pointing to her party dress.

"August ninth is my *birthday*," Rosie tells him in a confidential whisper. "I'm going to be *seven*."

"Well, happy birthday," says the man, his smile looking both happier and sadder than it did before. Mama squeezes her hand again.

The man says, "Are you going to have a party tonight?"

"*Yes*," says Rosie, and giggles. Mama giggles too, smiling at the man. "We're going to the park in Bristol!"

"On the number 60 bus?"

"Yes, the bus!" Rosie bounces up and down. "When will it be here?" Mama glances at her with a tiny frown, but asking the man isn't the same as asking Mama.

"Just about five minutes," he says. "I'm going on it too, but I'm getting off before you, in Warren."

"I like Warren! They have a big shoe store there!"

The man says to Mama, "A consumer already, eh?" Mama nods, smiling at him.

"Yes," the man says to Rosie. "I like Warren too. It's just the place to be, tonight."

Just then, the number 60 bus, silvery and shadowed, pulls into the space next to them with a moan of brakes and a hiss of doors. The grey man starts, and a little whimper of surprise escapes him; then he shakes himself like a dog trying to get warm. In the reflected light from the bus, the man's head has a pale blue sheen. People begin to come out the door.

Then he looks as if he's just remembered something, and he pulls a little toy animal out of his pocket. "May I give her a birthday present?" he asks Mama.

"That's so sweet, but it isn't necessary," she answers.

"Please," he says, "I'd like to."

"Well, all right."

"This is for you," he says, handing Rosie the toy.

She recognizes it immediately. "Mushroom the Dog!" she squeals.

"Mushroom is her favorite," says Mama. "What do you say?" She asks Rosie in her gentle-warning voice.

"Thank you very much," says Rosie.

"You're very welcome," says the man. The bus is almost empty now, and the grey man is going to be the first one to get on.

"Is it really, truly mine?" she asks. Then she feels silly; it's a *present*, after all.

"Yes," he says. He kneels down and looks her right in the eyes. "And no one will ever be able to take it from you."

He takes a deep breath, as if tasting the air. Then he straightens up and turns away from mother and daughter. Humming a sad tune to himself, he mounts the steps of the bus and disappears into the unknown depths within.

A friend told me about a media company threatening parents over a mural they painted on their daughter's bedroom wall. While I would have expected to be indignant, I was surprised by how fixated I became, rehearsing what I would say to company lawyers if I represented the parents.

I tried to imagine someone who becomes so obsessed with a plethora of small injustices that he goes a little mad, narrowing his life until it becomes nothing but his crusade against his personal monster. I wanted to show him from the outside, through the eyes of others who try and fail to understand him, covering the full spectrum from Violet to Rosie.

Mushroom the Dog is a character I dreamed up for my children's bedtime stories. He was a combination of truffle hound and gourmet chef, and was always being called upon to help out his friend, the restaurateur Alberto Funghi.

— KLS

Half a Degree

June 24, 2115
Elizabeth Fitzroy
66 Bosworth Court
Wayland, Massachusetts
Re: Estate of William Fitzroy

Dear Elizabeth:

This letter summarizes my research concerning your grandfather Williarr estate.

Where there are no surviving children, Massachusetts law provid that intestate property descends according to degrees of kinship. As tl sole granddaughter, you are two degrees of kinship removed from yoı grandfather. Since William was an only child, and your father and au both predeceased him, ordinarily you would be the sole heir of the estate.

However, the new claim of George Fitzroy complicates things. I Massachusetts, a clone is half-a-degree of kinship removed from the donc Since George is a clone of your late father, he stands half-a-degree of kinsh from your father, and consequently one-and-a-half degrees from yoı grandfather. Therefore he appears to be the heir-at-law to the entirety your grandfather's estate.

While we could contest this claim, the documentation of the cloning of George Fitzroy appears to be immaculate. The Massachusetts Supreme Judicial Court held, in *In re Estate of Plantage*, that clone kinship is identical to blood or adoptive kinship for inheritance purposes, excepting the difference in degree.

As a result, I do not believe that a challenge to George's inheritance of the estate would be successful. It would also be costly, and I cannot, in good conscience, counsel you to undertake it. Although we could threaten such a challenge in the hopes that George will settle with us, I think that George's attorney would expect to prevail without trial, and would probably refuse to negotiate.

I am sorry that I don't have better news for you. If I can be of any assistance, do not hesitate to contact me.

Very truly yours,

Francis Wall
Attorney at Law

July 1, 2115
Francis Wall, Esq.
100 Federal Street
Boston, Massachusetts

Dear Frank,

This is outrageous. I spent the last five years caring for my grandfather, and he promised that he would put me into his will. Why should his property go to a stranger?

It's even worse for my friend Edward. He grew *up* in my grandfather's house, for crying out loud. My grandfather was his *guardian*. But Edward gets nothing either. We've been going through my grandfather's papers, thousands of them, but there's nothing, no will, no adoption papers, *nothing*.

This George Fitzroy is a beach bum who never gave my grandfather the time of day. I don't know why my father had a clone made in the first place, but by the time George was an adult, he and Dad were doing god-knows-what in Provincetown. It's sick. He's no relative, not the way I was taught to use the word.

And isn't what George and my father were doing the same thing as incest? Doesn't the fact that they were committing incest make a difference?

Please find a way to challenge this thing. It's ridiculous!

Yours,

Elizabeth Fitzroy

♎

July 10, 2115
Elizabeth Fitzroy
66 Bosworth Court
Wayland, Massachusetts
Re: Estate of William Fitzroy

Dear Elizabeth:

Unfortunately, an oral promise by your grandfather William to name you as a devisee probably will not be regarded as a binding contract. We might also make a claim of compensation for your services caring for your grandfather, but the amount would be a small fraction of the estate's value.

I am sorry about your friend Edward's situation, but as you say, an adult has no claim on his former guardian's intestate property.

In answer to your other query, the 2089 amendments to the Massachusetts incest statutes expressly exempt clonal relationships from those provisions; consensual sexual relations with an adult clone are not incest. Further, even without those amendments, there are no statutes or case law preventing George's inheritance based on incest.

I am concerned that your preoccupation with this issue is leading you to such desperate speculation. I know that there is a lot of money involved, but sometimes it is best to accept the inevitable and move on.

If I can be of any additional help in this matter, please do not hesitate to call me.

Very truly yours,

Francis Wall
Attorney at Law

WHILE YOU WERE OUT

For: Frank
Date: 8/6/15
Time: 1:30
Caller: Eliz. Fitzroy

Message: Found something new in her grampa's papers. Says her grampa kept some secrets, and that the secrets kept secrets. (???) Please call ASAP.

Signed: *Mary*

♎

COMMONWEALTH OF MASSACHUSETTS

IN THE PROBATE COURT FOR

MIDDLESEX COUNTY

——————————————

In the matter of)
the Estate of)
William Fitzroy,)
deceased)

——————————————

MOTION
OF ELIZABETH FITZROY AND EDWARD LANCASTER

FOR DECLARATORY JUDGMENT AND

ORDER OF DISTRIBUTION

MOVANTS SAY:

1. On September 18, 2015, movants Elizabeth Fitzroy and Edward Lancaster were married in Middlesex county. (Marriage License, Exhibit A)

2. Movant Edward Lancaster is the documented clone of Henry Lancaster, deceased. (Clone Certification Affidavit, Exhibit B, and Certificate of Death, Exhibit C)

3. Henry Lancaster was the documented clone of William Fitzroy, the intestate in this matter. (Clone Certification Affidavit, Exhibit D)

4. Movant Edward Lancaster consequently stands one degree of kinship

from the intestate William Fitzroy, as per M.G.L. ch. 190, §§ 3-4.

5. There are no other heirs of William Fitzroy who stand one degree of kinship or less from the intestate.

6. Claimant George Fitzroy, as the clone of a child of William Fitzroy, stands one-and-a-half degrees of kinship from the intestate.

NOW, THEREFORE, MOVANTS PRAY THAT THIS COURT:

1. Declare Edward Lancaster to be the sole heir to the estate of William Fitzroy.

2. Dismiss all other claims to the estate of William Fitzroy, including, but not limited to, the claim of George Fitzroy.

3. Name movant Elizabeth Fitzroy Administrator of the Estate of William Fitzroy.

4. Grant movants such other relief as may be reasonable and lawful.

Submitted this 24th day of September, 2115

By Francis Wall
Attorney for Movants

Most people who speculate about the legal rights of clones seem to think that they'd either (1) be some sort of chattel, (2) have the same rights as someone unrelated to the "original", or (3) be wards of their originals. I wondered whether they might be viewed as blood relatives (indeed, the closest possible blood relatives). This led me to think about inheritance under intestate succession, which led to this story.

I had more fun than I probably should have with the character names.

— KLS

The Whole Truth Witness

If the jury had had any pity, they'd have waited a decent interval before returning the verdict. But the order to return flashed on Manny's thumbnail even before lunch had arrived at the café across the street from the courthouse. Elsa saw it and gave him a tense little nod before reaching for her bag; she glanced over at the client but didn't say a word.

Manny knew his paralegal was right: he ought to warn the client of just how bad it was going to be, but he hadn't the heart. So Pimentel got the full impact of the mammoth damage award in the courtroom itself. He bent forward as if punched in the stomach, a hollow wheeze escaping his mouth. On the way out of the building, he wouldn't look at them, and, Manny guessed, probably wouldn't pay his bill — probably *couldn't* pay it; the judgment was going to bankrupt him.

Manny and Elsa walked back to the office in the rain. Even in her high-heels, Elsa was about three-quarters Manny's height and forty percent his weight, and had to splatter beside him to keep up, making her even more visibly impatient than usual.

"That's the sixth case in a row," she said, twitching her umbrella back and forth.

"Don't start," said Manny.

"No, listen. You've got to stop taking cases where the other side has a Whole Truth witness. It's destroying your practice and your reputation."

He ground his teeth. "It's not my fault. You ought to have to notify someone before they speak to a Whole Truth witness."

"But you've tried that argument, no?"

"Yes."

"And you lost."

"*Yes.*"

"And even the Supreme Court — "

Manny made a helpless gesture with the arm holding the litigation bag, wondering whether she nagged her husband this way. "What do you suggest? That we avoid any case where Ed Ferimond is the opposing counsel, or where the other side is any decent-sized corporation? Not to mention most criminal cases?" He sidestepped a large puddle, only to land in another one. "Exactly what cases should I take?"

"You could do more divorces," said Elsa. Manny didn't answer; the words hung in the soggy air like a promise of eternal mud.

Dripping on the worn carpet of the office and mopping her face with a paper towel, Elsa checked the incoming messages with the no-nonsense efficiency that made her worth far more than he could afford to pay her. Most of the messages were confirmations of hearing dates or responses to discovery requests, but one was an inquiry from a new potential client: Tina Beltran, who had just been served with a summons and complaint from WorldWide Holdings, LLC. A copy of the complaint was attached to the message.

"Well, what do you know," said Manny, skimming the document and realizing that he'd missed lunch. "A civil suit under PIPRA, maybe even a case of first impression; well, well. Do you want to order out for sandwiches?"

"No, you should have a salad," said Elsa, heating water for a cup of tea and holding her hands over the first wisps of steam. He could see her hair starting to recover some of its frizz as it dried. "Case of first impression; is that good?"

"It could be. If it's a high-profile case, it might give us a reputation as experts and bring in more business later."

"If we win, you mean." Elsa started calling up menus from her favorite salad shacks.

"Yes. You know, I'd really rather have the pulled pork at Tomas's."

"I know that's what you'd really rather," she said, not deviating from the salad menus. "I don't suppose WorldWide Holdings has a Whole Truth witness?"

Manny skimmed down to the bottom of the pleading, seeing the name *Edward Ferimond, Attorney for Plaintiff.* He sighed. "I'm afraid it probably does."

♎

Although the medical malpractice case against Jerry Zucker did not involve a Whole Truth witness, it was just as hopeless in its own way. The plaintiff was spitting angry, even after seven months of discovery, and wanted to take Jerry for every cent he had. Manny supposed that disappointing plastic surgery would make anyone testy, but Helen Ishikawa was like a child holding her breath.

"Nelson says that Ishikawa isn't interested in a monetary settlement," Manny told Jerry over the phone.

"So you called to tell me that we have to go to trial?"

"Not necessarily. Nelson says that she wants you to fix the problem."

"Fix what problem?"

"Do the work the way she wanted it in the first place."

Jerry choked on whatever he was drinking. "What, she trusts me to do more surgery, after I supposedly ruined her body the last time?"

"It surprises me too; I can't say I'd trust you, myself."

Jerry didn't laugh. "And anyway, what she wanted wasn't really possible. I mean, some parts of the body just don't do certain things, you know? It's a matter of tissue structure and physics; I told her so at the time."

Manny skimmed his fingers back and forth across the desktop. "I wish you had used a good release and consent form."

"I'm doing it now, aren't I?"

"Yes, yes. Well, if there's no way of pleasing her, then we may have to go to trial after all. She won't consent to mediation."

There was a long pause. Manny could hear background sounds of fluid being poured into a glass. Then Jerry started to speak, stopped, started again: "Well . . . hm . . ." Manny waited, looking at his empty coffee cup.

Several noisy swigs or swallows later, the plastic surgeon said slowly, "I said that Ishikawa can't get what she wants by conventional techniques."

"You did say that, yes."

"But, well, there's an experimental technique — "

"Experimental?"

"Yes — involving TRUs."

Manny puffed air out through his nose, as if he were forestalling a sneeze. These days he detested the mention of TRUs; TRUs were the basis of the Whole Truth process and the consequent implosion of his trial practice.

He took a deep, slow breath, also through his nose. "How do TRUs help?"

"Well, in my early tests, they're able to sculpt tissue almost like clay, changing size, shape, texture, color. So if Ishikawa really wants her — "

Manny interrupted. "Have you ever tried this on an actual human being?"

"Only in highly controlled experiments with minor variations, part of the preliminary FDA approval process. Nothing as major as what she wants."

"So she'd be taking it on faith. Faith in you."

Jerry groaned. "Never mind; it was a stupid idea."

"Well, no, not necessarily. *Would* this technique work on Ishikawa, if you tried it? How certain are you?"

"Actually, given the sort of weird cosmetic changes she wants and where she wants them, I'm very certain."

"You don't want to buy yourself another malpractice lawsuit, after all."

"No, I'm certain."

Manny tapped out a salsa rhythm on the desk with his fingertips. "Let me call Nelson; maybe we can set something up."

♎

Tina Beltran turned out to be a nervous, fortyish woman with red hair who reminded Manny of a squirrel harassed by too many cats. "So I guess my case is hopeless," she said.

Manny steepled his fingers, giving Elsa a sidelong glance. She was taking notes, pretending not to have opinions; but he could tell, from the way her eyebrow twitched, that she agreed with the client.

"Not necessarily," he said. Elsa's eyebrow twitched again. "You never actually created a defragmenter, did you? You never wrote any code, assembled any modules, or anything like that?"

"Well, no, not to speak of. But Althoren —"

Manny's stomach rumbled at the same moment he interrupted her.

"Yes, thank you, I was getting to him. The only one who saw or heard you make any remarks about a defragmenter was Dieter Althoren?"

"Yes."

"There are no documents, electronic records, cold memory or other conversations about it?" An unbidden image of a sardine sandwich with mayonnaise popped into his head.

"No, but I intended — "

Manny held up his finger in a reliably commanding gesture; the finger reminded him of a sardine. "Actually I don't think I need to know what you intended, Ms. Beltran. Our concern should be with the evidence. Mr. Althoren was the only person there? And there were no other conversations?"

Beltran froze, as if she'd caught the sudden scent of a predator. Finally she said, "Yes, but he's enough, isn't he?"

The twitch in Elsa's eyebrow seemed to be attempting to send Morse code. Manny asked, "Do you mean, because of Whole Truth?"

"Well, obviously."

Now Elsa dropped her pretence of objectivity and stared at him the way she probably stared at her children when she caught them in a lie.

Manny folded his hands over his increasingly empty belly and spoke slowly to Beltran, avoiding Elsa's gaze. "I agree that the Whole Truth process gives us a disadvantage in the courtroom."

"Disadvantage?" Beltran chittered. "They'll believe every word he says!"

Inwardly Manny sighed. Too many client consultations reached this same impasse. His head inclined one way, then the other. "I'll admit it's a risk. But tell me, how strongly do you feel about this case?"

"How strongly do I feel?" Manny imagined the thrashing of Beltran's angry tail. "One: all I did was talk. Two: all I talked about was creating a defragmenter to reassemble media files with expired copyrights. *Expired* copyrights, Mr. Suarez! Three: this stupid lawsuit is by some holding company I never even heard of, for my life savings! How do I *feel*?"

"Well," said Manny, "I think a lot of people will feel the way you do about it — people on the jury, for example. Not a lot of people have even heard of the PIPRA statute. Once they understand what it is, well, it seems pretty compelling, doesn't it? Giant holding company bankrupts honest designer for talking about creating software to do something perfectly legal?"

Beltran chewed her lip rapidly. "So you don't think we should settle, Mr. Suarez?"

"Please call me Manny. Well, so far they haven't offered us any settlement. If they do, naturally we should consider it."

"We could offer a settlement ourselves."

Manny gave her his widest, hungriest smile. "Would you like to?"

Her beady eyes flashed. "No."

"Good," he said. "Because I think we can beat them."

After Tina Beltran left the office, Elsa stood in the doorway to the conference room, all sixty inches of her, fierce and birdlike, staring at Manny as if he were a shoplifter or graffiti artist.

"What?" asked Manny. Elsa didn't answer, but her eyes narrowed. He continued, "I'm starving. Do you want a sandwich?"

"You are a shameless, unprincipled opportunist," she said, sounding more like a crow than a songbird.

"You object to the sandwich?"

"I'm not talking about the goddam *sandwich*." Then, as if changing her mind, she glowered at his belly. "Anyway, you eat too much."

"Do you nag Felix this way?"

"*Felix* doesn't lie to people and build false hopes."

"Neither do I."

"Really?" she asked, speaking through her sharp little beak as she did at her most sarcastic. "After the last six cases, you expect to overcome the testimony of a Whole Truth witness?"

"It's possible," he said, not very convincingly.

Elsa stepped up to him so that her nose was about six inches from the bottom of his breastbone, and started poking her index finger into his chest with each word, as if pecking for worms. "You — " *Peck.* " — got — " *Peck.* " — her — " *Peck.* " — hopes — " *Peck.* " — up." *Peck, peck, peck.*

"Ow, stop it, get away. Look — " He rubbed his chest with his palm. "This is a test case for PIPRA. If we win it — "

"With what? Good intentions? Political sympathies of the jury? I can see it now: *Members of the jury, you should give a damn about little Tina Beltran and some complicated IP statute you never heard of.* Manuel Suarez waves his magic wand and everybody ignores the evidence."

"That's possible too." She glared at him. "There's a good chance that PIPRA is unconstitutional."

"And how many levels of appeal would it take to decide that point in her favor? Don't tell me that WorldWide isn't going to keep going until they run out of courts."

He tried to find a way around her through the doorway, but she blocked him. "Possibly all the way to the Supreme Court," he conceded.

"*Si*. And we know how much *that* costs, don't we? Do you imagine that that woman has anything like those resources?" If she'd really been a bird, she would have flown into his face.

"I'll think of something," Manny said. "I always think of something."

Elsa shook her head and marched out of the room.

"It doesn't look like it's going to work," Manny told Jerry Zucker. "She doesn't want the procedure when it's totally untested."

He could hear Jerry's sigh over the phone. "So we're back where we started from, aren't we?"

"Yes. We were pretty close, too. Nelson says that if you even had a few patients with major alterations or enhancements from your TRU process, Ishikawa might give it a go — he says she'd even drop the suit and sign a release."

There was a sound of something soft banging on something hard — possibly Jerry's fist on his desk, or maybe his forehead. "Hell."

"I don't suppose there's any way you could produce a confidential human subject, is there?" asked Manny.

"What?"

"Well, from what Nelson told me, I gather that Ishikawa would accept any successful subject, even one that wasn't, well, fully disclosed to the FDA."

"You're kidding; we're supposed to trust her with something like that? It's like giving a blackmailer the key to your diary."

"She seems to want this alteration very badly; we might be able to get her to sign a confidentiality agreement."

"Well, I'm sorry, but there is no such patient. I've been a good boy, and I haven't engaged in human experimentation without a go-ahead from the powers-that-be."

"Not even with a consent form?"

"Manny."

"Ah, well. It was worth a try. Looks like the courtroom for us."

"Not a lot of plastic surgeons on juries."

"No, I'm afraid not."

As he hung up, Manny wondered idly whether Jerry would be happy living in some other country and engaging in some other profession.

Probably not.

Then he looked up and saw Elsa, standing in the doorway of his office like a torch of righteousness. "Have you found some way not to cheat Tina Beltran?" she asked.

"It's nice to see you too, Elsa. I'm not cheating her."

Elsa began counting on her fingers. "No way to avoid the Whole Truth evidence. No way to cause jury nullification. No way to get a ruling on the law without bankrupting the client. Shall I go on?"

"I'll think of something, *chica*."

"Don't call me *chica*. You'll think of something, right. You have the gall to take that woman's money, and you have *nothing*. She deserves more than to put her hopes in one of your hallucinations!"

Manny froze, not breathing. He looked at Elsa as if he'd never seen her before. "Say that again."

"I said, she deserves more than to put her hopes into one of your — "

He interrupted her, grinning indecently. "Elsa, I love you."

"I'll tell Felix," she warned.

"Go ahead. I'll pay him a fair price for you; how much do you suppose he wants?"

"Do you want another finger in the chest?"

But Manny was chortling. "Listen, Elsa, listen. If I had, really had, a way of beating WorldWide, would you help me?"

"Of course I'd do that."

"No matter what it entailed?"

She folded her arms and raised an angular eyebrow. "What did you have in mind?"

♎

Dieter Althoren watched through his window as the creepy little car drove away through the canyons of January snow, chewing his lip until he was sure it wasn't coming back.

His parents had warned him about this. "Don't go along with it," Vatti had said. "You don't know what will happen to you. What will you do if they screw you up?" But he'd needed the money so badly; this job had been his last hope. And the doctors had been so sure, so confident; they'd said that the failure rate was so low. . . He tried to swallow in a dry throat, felt faint, and let himself drop onto the couch.

What to do? If he told Ed Ferimond what had happened, he'd lose his job, and he didn't believe for a damn minute that the lawyer or anybody else would help him. *But you signed a release*, they'd say. *We told you the risks, and you agreed to accept them. "Hold harmless," see? It says so right here.* Bastards.

Well, fine. He wasn't going to tell Ferimond or anybody else what had happened. When was he next seeing the son of a bitch? Not until April, to prepare for the stupid deposition. He'd tell the "whole truth and nothing but the truth," sure — hell, with those damn bugs in his head he couldn't do anything else — but he didn't have to tell anyone what they didn't ask.

♎

At jury selection, Manny behaved exactly the way Edward Ferimond expected him to behave. He asked each juror what she knew about the Protection of Intellectual Property Revision Act, how it was drafted, who sponsored it, who the lobbyists were. He mentioned WorldWide's name as often as he could. Ferimond, who had the grace, beauty and haughtiness of an Abyssinian cat, made frequent objections, lazily accusing him of biasing the jury and turning a simple civil suit into a political trial. Judge Rackham seemed bored by both Manny's questions and Ferimond's objections; some objections she sustained, but most she overruled, since the jurors' opinions about PIPRA were potentially sources of bias.

But Ferimond did not seem to find anything objectionable in Manny's tedious repetition of the same question to each and every juror: "Can I count on you to rely on your own assessment of the evidence, rather than allowing someone else to tell you which witnesses are truthful, lying, or just crazy?" Of course they'd all said yes.

In pretrial conference, Ferimond had looked genuinely put out when Manny declined to stipulate to the reliability of testimony from a Whole Truth witness, although he never had and never would.

So here Ferimond was, his body language conveying how many better things he had to do, questioning Eleanor Moncrief, Ph.D., a plump woman in a flattering blue suit and matching eyes, qualifying her as an expert, and taking her through the familiar territory of the Whole Truth enhancement procedure.

"The Tissue Redirection Units alter pathways in the parts of the brain associated with memory and volition," said Dr. Moncrief in a surprising contralto. "The TRUs are injected in a saline solution, effect their changes in the appropriate neural tissue and then decompose into trace minerals that pass out of the system. From injection to elimination, the procedure takes about 48 hours."

"And what," yawned Ferimond, "is the result of this procedure on the behavior of the subject?"

"There are two primary results. First, the subject has total recall of all events occurring after the procedure. Second, he becomes incapable of telling a knowing falsehood."

"How long do these behavioral changes last?"

"They are permanent, until the procedure is reversed or some organic event takes place, such as degradation of tissue with age or illness."

"In the case of Dieter Althoren," said Ferimond, seeming to regain some interest in what he was doing. "When was the procedure performed?"

"June 23rd of last year," said Dr. Moncrief.

"Did you perform the procedure yourself?"

"Well, my med-tech did the actual injection. But apart from that, yes, I did."

"So far as you are aware, has the procedure been reversed?"

"Not so far as I know."

"So, doctor, would it be fair to say that anything said by Mr. Althoren relating to any event occurring after June 23rd of last year would be truthful and accurate?"

"Objection, Your Honor." Although addressing the judge, Manny looked right at the jury. He rose with exaggerated difficulty. "Counsel is asking the witness to opine on a matter of credibility. The jury determines whether a witness is truthful." He nodded approvingly to the jurors, then sat down slowly.

"Sustained."

Ferimond gave a long-suffering sigh. "Let me rephrase, doctor. Have there been tests during the last twenty years of subjects' accuracy and credibility following the Whole Truth procedure?"

"There have been dozens of studies."

"What is the percentage of subjects who display, within normal tolerances, perfect truthfulness and accuracy?"

"According to the literature reviews I've seen, that figure is 97.5 percent, plus or minus two percent."

Ferimond did not quite smirk, but he looked at Manny as if to say, *Why waste your time?* "No more questions."

Manny rose as Ferimond sat. He addressed the witness with his friendliest face. "Doctor Moncrief, where does that two-and-a-half percent failure rate come from?"

She smiled back. "A tiny fraction of pathways do not respond as predicted. For most subjects, the incidence of such pathways is so small that the results are the same. But for just a few, the cumulative effect of unaltered pathways results in unaltered behaviors."

"These subjects have either inaccurate memories, or are still able to lie?" asked Manny.

"Yes, but I must emphasize that you are talking about one subject out of forty."

He nodded. "I see. Now, when you speak of the memories being accurate, you're speaking of memories as *perceived* by the subject, yes? I mean to say, if the subject's eyes or ears were not working properly, the subject would recall sights and sounds as garbled by his senses, wouldn't he?"

She nodded too. "Yes, he would."

Manny adopted the tone of a curious student. "And also our memories are affected by our own attitudes, aren't they? If a person associates dogs with violence, he might remember a dog he saw as being violent when that dog wasn't actually violent, isn't that so?"

"Yes," Moncrief responded slowly. "Within limits."

"What limits?"

"Well, if he had time to see what the dog was really doing, I don't believe he would manufacture things that weren't there. For example, he wouldn't say that there was blood dripping from the fangs when it wasn't."

"But if the dog actually made a friendly move, the subject might interpret it and report it differently, yes?"

"Yes, I think that's right."

Manny nodded. "One more question. If a person is already subject to garbled perceptions, for reasons of mental illness, drug use, brain damage or other causes, the Whole Truth process doesn't actually cure those things, does it?"

She frowned for a second, then answered. "No, but there are other procedures that we can employ to effect changes like that."

He nodded again, looking eager to please. "Surely, surely, but you'd have to know of such conditions, wouldn't you, before you could cure them?"

"We would."

Manny smiled gratefully and sat down again, beaming at the whole room as if he were planning on treating them all to drinks and dinner.

Dieter Althoren, blonde, 28, thin as a rope, earnest of expression, was sworn as the plaintiff's next and last witness. Silkily Ferimond led Althoren through his visit to Tina Beltran's office a mere two weeks after undergoing the Whole Truth procedure, what the room looked like, what she was wearing, the color of her nail polish. Then they padded together through the conversation itself, stopping at every breath and turn of phrase in Beltran's manner, how he asked her about defragmenters, how she said she was planning on writing one, how he offered to pay her for a copy and she agreed.

Throughout the direct examination, Manny quietly arranged and rearranged a few coins on top of the counsel's table, as if not noticing even that Althoren was speaking. When Ferimond said, "Your witness," Manny stood with even more difficulty than before, shuffling his papers in a doddering, confused manner. He glanced up apologetically at the witness and took a full twenty seconds to find the page he was looking for. The foolish fat man, that was Manny.

"Good morning, Mr. Althoren," he said, smiling.

"Good morning, sir."

"Let's see, you and I haven't met before today, have we?"

Althoren gave Manny a knowing grin, as if spotting a trap. "You took my deposition, Mr. Suarez."

Manny touched his forehead like a man who's left his keys in the car. "That's right, that's right, thank you for reminding me. The deposition. That was in March of this year, wasn't it?"

"April, Mr. Suarez." Althoren's grin broadened.

"Of course. Dear me." Manny shook his head ruefully. "But at any rate, we can say with confidence that you and I hadn't met before the deposition, can't we?"

Althoren's expression changed. He seemed reluctant to speak, but, as if unable to stop himself, said, "I'm afraid we can't say that."

Manny's eyebrows rose, and he cocked his head. "We can't?"

Althoren's voice dropped noticeably. "No, sir. We met in January, at my house."

Manny frowned and put down his paper; then he opened, consulted, and closed a leather-bound calendar. Out of the corner of his eye he saw a confused look ripple across Ferimond's face. Manny frowned even more deeply, making impressive bulges in his face. "We did? In January?"

"Yes, sir."

"I came to your house?"

"You did."

"Was I alone?"

"No sir, your paralegal, Ms. Morales, was there too." Althoren gestured at Elsa.

"Ah." Manny chewed his lip, glancing at Elsa in apparent confusion. Then he spoke as if humoring someone who was making an elaborate joke. "Well, I imagine if it was winter, I must have looked pretty awful, eh? Not my best time of year."

Althoren looked even more unhappy. "You could say that. You had that awful green skin."

Manny looked taken aback, then relaxed. "Green — ah, you mean that I looked peaky, right? Green, like I wanted to throw up?"

Althoren shook his head. "No, I mean emerald green. Green, like my neighbor's lawn."

Manny's mouth gaped; then he said, "My skin?"

"Yes."

"Emerald green?"

"That's right." Manny turned to the jury; all of them were examining his copper complexion; several wore puzzled expressions.

"My hair wasn't green too, was it?"

Ferimond, who seemed just to have realized what was going on, interrupted as smoothly as he could. "Objection. What is the relevance of these questions?"

Judge Rackham, though, was scrutinizing Althoren and did not even look up. "Overruled. You may answer, Mr. Althoren."

"No sir, you had no hair, and you had antennae growing out of your head." One of the spectators snorted; Rackham gave the man a warning look.

Manny swallowed, took a drink of water, and swallowed again. Then he said weakly, "What color were the antennae? Green?"

"No, they were bright red, and they wiggled."

There were more guffaws in the courtroom. Rackham and Ferimond both glared, though for different reasons. Manny silently mouthed the word *wiggled*, raised his hands in apparent helplessness, then said, as if it were an offhand remark, "Well, Ms. Morales didn't have green skin, did ıe?"

"No, she didn't."

"That's good. Do you remember what she was wearing?"

"How could I forget? She had no shirt on."

"No shirt on? In January?"

"No shirt on under her coat."

"Oh. Do you mean she sat in your house in her brassiere?"

"No, she never sat, and she was bare-chested." Ferimond looked wildly : Elsa, who seemed merely puzzled.

Manny's face took on a pained expression, as if pleading with Althoren) talk sensibly. "Mr. Althoren, have you any idea why Ms. Morales should ɔme into a stranger's house half-dressed?"

Althoren was sweating. "She said it was so that her wings wouldn't urt."

Manny's mouth stayed open for five seconds. Ferimond's stayed open ınger; "emerald green" might not have been a bad description of his own .ce just then. Manny said, "Her — her wings?"

"Yes," said Althoren, closing his eyes.

"Did you, er, see those wings?"

"I did."

"What did they look like?"

"They were white and feathery, and about three feet long."

"Um." Manny stared at Elsa, who stared back and shrugged. Then, as ' trying to take command of a crazy situation, Manny said, "Come now, ɔuldn't these wings have been a costume?"

"No sir. She flapped them."

"Flapped. She didn't fly, did she?"

"No, she said she hadn't learned how yet."

There was a roar of laughter from the spectators and several members f the jury. Judge Rackham pounded her gavel for order.

Manny tossed his papers onto the desk and said, "Your honor, I really ınnot continue with this witness. I have no more questions." He sat down.

Judge Rackham turned to Ferimond. "Re-direct?"

Ferimond banished the dazed expression from his face, forced himself) stand, and managed to say, "Judge, I'd like to request a brief recess before ıy re-direct examination."

Rackham's face said, *I'll bet.* Her voice said, "Very well, you can have venty minutes. Mr. Althoren, you will remain under oath during the recess."

Ferimond gestured angrily for Althoren to follow him, and the two of them left the courtroom. The jury filed out into their lounge, some bewildered, some amused. Manny whistled tunelessly, looking through a reference book he'd brought for show. Elsa rolled her eyes. Tina Beltran, who was as confused by Althoren's testimony as anyone, leaned towards Manny and whispered, "What was *that* all about?"

"Hush," said Manny, taking out his watch and laying it on the table. "We'll see."

Exactly twenty minutes later, Ferimond and Althoren reentered the courtroom. Ferimond looked aggrieved; he glared at Manny before sitting.

When the jury had re-entered, Rackham asked, "Re-direct examination, Mr. Ferimond?"

Ferimond stood; through gritted teeth he said, "No judge, we rest."

"Very well. Mr. Suarez, you may present your first witness."

Manny stood more easily this time. "Actually, Your Honor, we'd like to waive the presentation of Defendant's case and proceed immediately to our closing argument."

Rackham looked startled, the jury puzzled, Ferimond aghast. "Mr. Suarez," said Rackham, "you're not going to present any evidence at all?"

"No, Judge. Since Plaintiff has the burden of proof, his failure to present sufficient evidence is grounds for the jury to find in our favor. As I do not believe Plaintiff has proved his case, I see no reason to bother refuting it."

"Are you moving for a directed verdict, then?"

"No, Judge, but thank you for asking. I just want to talk to the jury."

Rackham tapped her fingernails on the bench. "I'm not going to indulge you if you change your mind later, Mr. Suarez."

"Understood, Your Honor."

"I expect that you'll want a continuance to prepare your closing argument?" She glanced over at her clerk, who was already checking the calendar.

Manny said, "No ma'am. We have half the day left, and I'm ready now."

Rackham consulted the file summary in front of her. "Um, I don't think we've settled the jury instructions yet, have we?"

"Actually, Your Honor, we've read plaintiff's proposed jury instructions and we're content to let those stand. They're fine. But I'm ready for my closing."

The judge nodded. Manny thought she might be thinking about her docket.

Ferimond sputtered, "Your Honor, this is ridiculous! We're hardly ready for closing. We expected Defendant to present a case!"

"That's up to him, Counsel."

"But our own closing isn't ready."

"Then *you* can have a continuance after Mr. Suarez has finished." Ferimond's mouth worked, but nothing came out. Rackham sighed. "Please be seated, Mr. Ferimond. Mr. Suarez, you may proceed."

"Permission to approach the jury?"

"Granted."

Manny wandered over to the jury box, shaking his head. "For a thousand years, juries have had the role of deciding the credibility of witnesses. Everyone knows there are excellent liars in the world, and that no one is a perfect judge of character. We have faith that twelve citizens, using their own wits and working together, can tell the liars from the truth-tellers.

"But now a few clever engineers invent a device which, they say, takes that job away from you. They say that a witness who's had the Whole Truth process cannot forget, cannot lie, that anything he says must be true. They would have this machine tell you what to believe.

"But that is not the way our system is works. It is still *you*, the jury, who determine whether a witness is telling the truth. Neither I, nor Mr. Ferimond, nor the judge herself can tell you what to believe, and neither can a collection of TRUs. Even those who say they believe in the Whole Truth process admit that it can commit an error. I say that your own common sense tells you when an 'error' is present.

"It is possible that I have green skin and wiggling red antennae, or at least that I had them in January. It is possible that Ms. Morales, a married woman with two children, walked into a Mr. Althoren's house, bared her chest to him and flapped a set of white angel's wings. If you believe those things, then you should also believe Mr. Althoren's other testimony, and hold that Tina Beltran engaged in the conspiracy of which she is accused. Otherwise, you should find that Mr. Ferimond and WorldWide Holdings have failed to prove their case."

Manny sat down. It was the shortest closing argument he'd ever made.

♎

The next morning, Ferimond delivered a closing that was, in Manny's opinion, a tactical blunder. He focused entirely on Althoren's testimony in direct examination, the details of the conversation with Tina Beltran, and how those facts proved the illegal conspiracy prohibited by PIPRA. He did not address the peculiarities of Althoren's cross-examination testimony at all; indeed, he behaved as if the cross-examination had never occurred.

The judge's jury instructions were tilted towards WorldWide, of course, since Manny had not bothered arguing them. If he lost, Beltran might sue him for malpractice.

But the jury was out for less than a half-hour before they returned a verdict in favor of the defendant. Manny rose to ask for statutory attorney's fees.

After accepting Tina Beltran's excited hug, as he and Elsa walked back to the office, this time in giddy sunshine, Manny pulled a personal check out of his jacket pocket. "Three months' bonus," he said.

Elsa glanced down at the check without touching it. "Four," she said.

"What?"

"Four. You owe me more."

"I thought you only wanted two."

"That was before I saw the scars."

"What?"

"Scars. On my back. Zucker promised there wouldn't be any, but there they are, one on each side."

"I'm sorry."

"You should be; the whole thing is practically sexual harassment. But just pay for the cosmetic surgery and we'll call it even. I'm thinking of suing him for malpractice myself. Goddam pin feathers."

Most people don't understand that trials are designed not to determine the truth, but to measure the strength of the evidence. But what do you do in a world where one type of evidence universally trumps all others?

This story is based on an old trickster myth, which I first heard in the form of "Weezie and the Moonpies" by the delightful Bill Harley. In Harley's version, two boys contrive to avoid the vengeance of a local bully by convincing their truthful but guileless little sister that a number of magical things have happened. She reports these events to the bully along with the bad news that would provoke his wrath, and naturally he believes none of it.

— KLS

EXCEPTIONALISM

State of Michigan
Supreme Court

SPARTACUS MILLER,
Plaintiff-Petitioner-Appellant,
-v-
ROLAND CARVER, individually and in his capacity as Chief of Police of the City of Ann Arbor, et. al.,
Defendants-Respondents-Appellees.

BEFORE THE ENTIRE BENCH
Opinion of the Court by Justice WHEELWRIGHT.

These appeals arise from two separate actions. Plaintiff Spartacus Miller sued the various defendants in the Circuit Court for Washtenaw County, alleging false imprisonment and battery, and petitioning for a writ of *habeas corpus*. In another action before the Probate Court, plaintiff petitioned for guardianship, declaratory judgment of the validity of a conveyance, and authorization to terminate life support.

Summary judgment was entered against plaintiff in both actions, which judgments were separately affirmed by the Court of Appeals. We granted plaintiff's petition for leave to appeal, consolidating the cases on our own motion due to their common issues of law and fact.

The plaintiff is a chimpanzee (*Pan troglodytes*), intellectually enhanced by neurosurgical and electronic interventions. Noah Miller purchased the plaintiff some fifteen years ago, and later performed the various interventions himself, as well as training and educating the plaintiff. The evidence adduced on discovery suggests that the relationship between Noah and the plaintiff after the enhancements resembled that of parent and child.

During the six months prior to these lawsuits, Noah Miller executed a number of facially valid documents: a recorded deed of gift, creating a joint tenancy in real property between himself and the plaintiff; applications for checking, savings and investment accounts in the joint names of Noah and Spartacus Miller; a durable power of attorney naming the plaintiff as Noah's agent; a document entitled "Manumission Papers," purporting to "free" the plaintiff from his "bondage" to Noah; and a petition to the Probate Court, asking that the plaintiff be named as Noah's guardian. Noah contrived to file these instruments without revealing the fact that Spartacus Miller is not human.

Two days after filing the guardianship petition, Noah voluntarily underwent the so-called Selective Neural Erasure Process (SNEP), which permanently deactivates certain functions in the brain and has the effect of rendering the patient unconscious and intellectually inert. He assembled the equipment for this process himself, and there is no evidence that plaintiff took any part in it.

Five days after that, Samuel Farmer, a neighbor, visited the Miller home in order to borrow some lawn tools. Farmer knew that a chimpanzee resided in the home, but apparently was unaware of plaintiff's enhancements and was surprised when it was the plaintiff who answered the door. The plaintiff communicates only through sign language, which Farmer did not recognize. Finding Noah Miller unconscious and connected to medical apparatus, Farmer believed there was an emergency and contacted the police. The responding officers also did not understand the plaintiff's attempts to communicate, believing the plaintiff to be a pet. Noah was taken to a hospital, while the plaintiff was impounded.

Miller's attorney discovered the situation and located the plaintiff. The Animal Control office refused to release him. Subsequently counsel filed these actions on the plaintiff's behalf.

In his suits before the Circuit Court, the plaintiff alleged that the officers touched and then confined him without privilege or consent, constituting a battery and false imprisonment under common law, and continued to imprison him without authority, justifying the issue of a writ of *habeas corpus*. In his action in Probate Court, the plaintiff claimed: (1) that the documents executed by Noah Miller are valid and enforceable, making plaintiff the joint owner of various assets; (2) that plaintiff should be appointed Noah's legal guardian; and (3) that Noah, having no meaningful "quality of life", should be euthanized.

For all claims except the last one, the courts below held that the plaintiff, as a non-human, has no legal rights of any kind. Consequently he would have no right to recover in tort, no right to *habeas* relief, no ownership of property and no capacity to act as either agent or guardian. The refusal to order euthanasia was based on its continuing illegality under Michigan statute.

On appeal, the plaintiff argues that his demonstrable intelligence and ability to communicate entitle him to the same rights any human being would have. He further claims that Noah Miller, having no longer any consciousness or intellectual capacity, is no longer meaningfully "human", and that his life can be terminated as one would dispose of a sick animal.

This is a case of first impression, not only in Michigan but in all U.S. courts, concerning both the enhancement of chimpanzee intelligence and the SNEP procedure.

No statute grants legal rights to non-human animals, and prior attempts to obtain such rights though litigation have failed. Most courts addressing the question have relied primarily on precedent and tradition: humans have used animals as natural resources from time immemorial, and courts are reluctant to outlaw centuries of practice through judicial fiat.

Plaintiff points out, however, that the extant cases, to the extent that they reason at all, rely on the necessary linkage between rights and duties. A human being, able to assert rights against others, is also subject to duties to others. Humans are, in other words, "moral actors." Alone among animals, they can choose right or wrong action and be held accountable for those actions. Non-human animals, by contrast, are capable of no such moral choice and are not held so accountable. We may destroy a dangerous animal in order to protect persons or property, but we do not do so based on any moral culpability on the animal's part.

Plaintiff asserts that this reasoning supports his claims. He maintains that he is capable of moral choice and fidelity to his obligations, that he can be held to duties to others, and that consequently he should be able to assert rights against others.

Defendants maintain that the issue of moral culpability and connected legal rights applies to the species as a whole, not to individuals separately. We do not, they argue, assess the moral abilities of each particular human being, but rather presume rights to exist in the case of all members of *Homo sapiens*. Thus, they say, we should not assign legal rights to an animal unless its entire species is capable of moral choice. Since the plaintiff has not claimed to be a member of a new species, and since *Pan troglodytes*, as a group, has no such ability, they say that the plaintiff, as a member of that class, has no rights.

But this is incomplete. Courts often impose duties and recognize rights in individuals as exceptions to their class. Minors generally have no obligation to honor contracts, but exceptional minors seeking emancipation who demonstrate the requisite abilities become adults by court order, taking on those obligations. Adults who become mentally incompetent similarly may lose those same duties, also by court order.

Thus we think we have the ability to treat the plaintiff as an individual rather than a member of his species, and to err on the side finding him "human" if that is warranted.

For the foregoing reasons, we rule that the plaintiff, if he can demonstrate the capacity for cognition, moral accountability and fidelity to duty that he has claimed, is legally a person entitled to the rights ordinarily accorded to an adult human.

On the issue of euthanasia, however, the case stands on different footing. We acknowledge that the affidavits appear to confirm that Noah Miller has no consciousness or mental state as we understand it, and no significant chance of recovering them. The parts of his brain that would normally generate what we think of as "personality" are inert. One expert expressed the view that someone who voluntarily undergoes the SNEP process has, to all intents and purposes, committed suicide.

But Noah Miller is alive. His body is fully functional, as are those parts of his brain that maintain respiration, heartbeat, etc. So long as he is fed, hydrated and otherwise cared for, the experts opine that he is likely to live for years.

While Michigan statutes authorize "do-not-resuscitate" orders and advance directives, they do not authorize guardians to make such decisions unilaterally. Noah Miller, in the course of authorizing multiple powers for the plaintiff, did not convey the power to terminate Noah's life. In any case, Noah's condition does not match any of those in which the statute would authorize any such action.

The plaintiff maintains that a human body without its personality is not a "person." He says that such a body is incapable of honoring legal duties and has no moral culpability. He argues that the same logic which defines him as a person with legal rights now excludes Noah from those rights.

But this is not the law. While duties and legal obligations have been lifted from humans due to diminished intellectual capacity, fundamental human rights never have. There remains a presumption that human beings have rights, and this presumption is not rebutted by minority, intoxication, or even a persistent vegetative state.

Consequently Noah Miller has a right to remain alive, and the plaintiff, if he succeeds in becoming Noah's guardian, will have a duty to keep him alive, safe and comfortable, to the extent possible.

The judgment of the Probate Court denying permission to terminate Noah's life is affirmed. All other judgments of the Probate and Circuit Courts are reversed. The case is remanded to the Circuit Court for trial on the issue of the plaintiff's capacity.

IT IS SO ORDERED.

This story is a parody of a supposedly rigorous philosophical argument I saw on C-SPAN 2 several years ago. I recognize, of course, the similarities to both Heinlein's 'Jerry Was a Man' and the Twilight Zone episode 'I, Robot.' They're not deliberate, but there was no way of avoiding them.

The appellate judicial opinion is a form of writing I can do in my sleep, having spent the first year after law school doing almost nothing else. Although not exploited here, it lends itself very well to narrative dissonance: the judge is so limited in what she is allowed to say or even notice that the reader cannot help but feel the gap. To those who are interested, I recommend comparing the Supreme Court's decision in Hannsberry v. Lee (1940) to Lorraine Hannsberry's Raisin in the Sun, based on the same set of facts.

— KLS

Life of the Author Plus Seventy

The cab driver overcharged me on my way to sign the contract with Catskill. Okay, he charged me what the meter in the cab said, but the meter was wrong. I told him so, pointing out that the distance from the airport to Catskill Features, Inc. was exactly 25.3 km on the map. He said the routes were different. I said the routes were the same. He said I didn't know shit about driving. I leaned in to try to reset the meter to recalculate the route, but he put his big hand on my wrist.

"Fella," he said. "Is it worth getting into a fight over a few bucks?"

I paid him and got out. I didn't need to make trouble today.

Taking a job with Catskill Features as a staff writer in their Creative Cartoons department might have seemed like a victory to some people. First step on the road to media greatness! Generous salary! Luxurious benefits! Industry influence! But for me, it was a defeat. I'd been failing to make a living as a writer ever since I quit at Pascals, Winkle, Davis & Furlong. Well, okay, "quit" isn't precisely accurate; but I was going to quit anyway. I was pretty good at the work, just a little unorthodox for their taste. In my defense, if they'd waited for me to quit, I wouldn't have left all those insulting notes in the client files before I left.

In the intervening years I'd sold a few dozen short stories and one novel, but *Harriman's Loophole* seemed to have been read by no one except a reviewer with a migraine. The advance was only $14,000, and the royalties didn't earn out. I never spent any of it (I was living off my savings), but shoved it into a custodial investment account with the Neighborhood Bank of Tannersville, for someone else to worry about. You know how some people save the first quarter or dollar they earned, put it in a picture frame and hang it over the toaster? Not that I ever looked at it; it seemed a reminder of how my career had stalled. I preferred to forget it was there.

About five years after it came out, I went to the public library in Tannersville to check on their copy of *Harriman's Loophole* (which I'd asked them to buy). The list of past due dates was empty. No one had checked out the novel, not once since it had arrived. You'd think the few people I called friends could have made an effort for show.

So I checked it out myself and took it home with me, just so the damn list would have at least one borrowing date in it. A like-new copy of *Harriman's Loophole* by Eric Weiss, sitting proudly on my desk. Or maybe it was my kitchen table. Of course I already had about thirty pristine, unbought, unread copies of the novel. One more was scarcely noticeable. In fact, I didn't notice; I forgot, which was the problem. Part of the problem.

The HR guy from Catskill was Matthew Johnston, who looked like he advertised toothpaste for a living. The contract he handed me, amid the Persian rugs and "signed" photos of cartoon characters, was pretty thick; it reminded me of a commercial loan agreement from the old days.

Most people would have checked the salary figure on the first page, asked about the health plan and the vacation days, and signed quickly so as to get an early-bird view of their cubicle. Not me. Back at Pascals Winkle, I had a reputation for two things: close reading of documents, and finding hidden loopholes. Sure, all lawyers are supposed to be able to do that. But I could find negative implications the way a painter can find negative space in a composition.

"Sorry about this," I said, slowly turning from page four to page five. "Old habits die hard."

"No need to be sorry," Johnston said. "Legal puts so much work into these, it's nice to see that at least somebody reads them."

Then I looked up from the contract. "Wait, the copyrights are in my name? These won't be works for hire?"

"That's right," said Johnston. "But we get an exclusive, unlimite license, with full sublicensing power and agency authority to grant oth permissions."

I scanned down. "I see that. So you have all the rights you would ha if you bought the copyrights, except that I'm still technically the owner."

"Basically."

What, I wondered, was the point of doing it this way? I read on:

> In order to preserve the value of Catskill's various license rights und this Agreement, you agree to allow Catskill to place you in Preservati Hibernation, on the earliest of the following events:
>
> 1. You are diagnosed with an illness, condition or injury that is more tha 50% likely to cause your death within two years, and the treatmen prescribed fail to lengthen your prognosis after six months;
> 2. You are diagnosed with an illness, condition or injury that is mo than 50% likely to cause your death within two years, and you elect decline such treatments; or
> 3. You attain an age that is 90% of your Actuarially Determined Li Expectancy.

I read it three times. Then I said, "Catskill wants to put me i hibernation?"

"Only when you're in danger of dying," said Johnston.

"But *why*?"

"Well," Johnston said, putting his hands behind his head and leanir back in his leather chair. "If we took the things you write as works-fo hire, then the copyrights last for 90 years, maybe 120. But if you retai copyright and we and act only as a licensee, then the rights last for 70 yea after the end of your life. And if you're in Preservative Hibernation . . . He trailed off.

I don't know whether it took me a few seconds to see the point. "M death doesn't occur," I said. "My copyrights never expire, and — "

"And therefore, neither do our licenses."

"You — But who cares? Will Catskill even *exist* by that time?"

"Doesn't matter," said Johnston, shrugging with his hands still behin his head. "The longer lasting the right, the more valuable it is as propert And we don't need to wait to use it. The anticipated future value something we can sell to speculators right now or pledge against loans fc operating capital."

"So —" I stopped, then started again. "So, how long am I giving you permission to keep me in hibernation?"

"It's on the next page. Until a method of treatment becomes available to make it reasonably likely that you will not die within ten years."

"What if that never happens?"

"There's a maximum limit fixed at 500 years."

"You're joking. You want to be able to freeze me for five centuries?"

He shrugged again. "You don't have to work for us, after all."

That was true enough. Except that I did have to. If I wanted to make my living by writing instead of practicing law, Catskill was pretty much my only option. *My only option until I sell the big novel,* I told myself. But I already knew that "until I sell the big novel" would probably last longer than the Hibernation.

It wasn't so bad. The other writers, the artists and CGI specialists at Catskill were fun people. Turned out I had an office, not just a cubicle, that opened onto a state-of-the-art creative consultation room, where we could play with simulations, storyboards and scenarios to our hearts' content. The coffee was good, too. The hours were long, and often we had weekend work, but it was exciting and sometimes hilarious.

Eventually I became the lead writer for Constance the Cormorant, one of Catskill's most popular recurring characters. My salary went up. I still didn't know very many people outside of work, though. My parents had been dead for a decade, and I had no love life. The next novel barely got started, which was hardly surprising. It's hard to switch from *Constance's Mussel Tea Party* to literary masterpieces, if that's what the novel would have been. But the work was satisfying, and I had nothing to complain about.

Then, about six years later, I got this message one night when I'd come home late and was about to go to bed:

To: Eric Weiss
From: J3
Re: Library Fines
Date: February 23, 2107

Dear Mr. Weiss:

You still have not returned *Harriman's Loophole*, which you borrowed from the Tannersville Public Library on January 5, 2097. Under current law, library fines left unpaid double after each successive year. As a result, your original $100 fine has now reached $102,400. Please pay this amount immediately.

Yours truly,

J3

I stared at the message hanging in the air over my kitchen table. I remembered taking *Harriman's Loophole* out from the library a few years before I went to work for Catskill. I *thought* I remembered returning it, but with all the copies occupying my house like hotel guests, I easily could have missed one. Still, one hundred and two thousand dollars? I replied:

To: J3
From: Eric Weiss
Re: Library Fines
Date: February 24, 2107

Dear J3,

This is the first message I have received concerning any sort of late fines. I would be happy to return the book. Indeed, I have extra copies I can provide. I would also be happy to pay the initial fines. But you must understand that I cannot pay inflated late fees when I was not notified of the original fine.

Sincerely yours,

Eric Weiss

The answer came back within less than a minute:

To: Eric Weiss
From: J3
Re: Library Fines
Date: February 24, 2107

Dear Mr. Weiss:

Thank you for your message!

We are very sorry that you do not find our communications systems satisfactory. We take all complaints seriously. Rest assured that we will investigate your concerns.

Thank you for your willingness to pay your fine! You can use any of your available credit links.

Thank you for informing us that you have additional overdue copies of *Harriman's Loophole.* If you will inform us of the exact number, we will multiply the fines accordingly. Your cooperation is appreciated.

All borrowers are presumed to know the due date of their books, and therefore are presumed to know when fines have accumulated. The accumulation formula is a matter of public record, and can be found at municipalcollections.j3.cap.

Yours truly,

J3

I got up and paced the kitchen for a few minutes. Then I found a piece of paper and wrote the words *Stupid AI!* over and over until I filled the page. That calmed me down a little. I got a cup of coffee and started again:

To: J3
From: Eric Weiss
Re: Library Fines
Date: February 24, 2107

Dear J3,

I don't think you understood me.

I do not have additional overdue copies of *Harriman's Loophole.* I own 30 copies of that book. They belong to me. I was merely offering to give one of the them to the library as a show of good faith.

And I say again, I am not paying one dollar of the late fees.

Yours,

Eric Weiss

Again, the reply was absurdly fast:

To: Eric Weiss
From: J3
Re: Library Fines
Date: February 24, 2107

Dear Mr. Weiss:

Thank you for your message!

We are very sorry that you do not find our analysis of your communications satisfactory. We take all complaints seriously. Rest assured that we will investigate your concerns.

Thank you for informing us of the number of overdue books! Based on this information, your total fine is now $3,072,000. You can use any of your available credit links, or pay cash in person.

We are sorry that you do not intend to pay your late fees. Please understand that failure to pay such fines can result in civil actions and/or criminal prosecutions against you.

Yours truly,

J3

I put down the coffee cup and walked around the table. At midnight, I sent:

To: J3
From: Eric Weiss
Re: Library Fines
Date: February 25, 2107

Who is J3?

Best,

Eric Weiss

The response:

To: Eric Weiss
From: J3
Re: Library Fines
Date: February 25, 2107

Dear Mr. Weiss:

Thank you for your message!

J3 is the latest innovation in public institution customer-service software. It is able to handle tens of millions of customer issues at a time, but never loses track of individual personalities and needs.

A unique heuristic analysis protocol and multilinked database make it possible for J3 to engage in intelligent decision-making and cheerful, pleasant conversation with the customer.

Thank you for asking about J3!

Yours truly,

J3

I poured my cold coffee into the sink. There was no point arguing. I'd have to write to the Library itself.

I tried. The response came back signed by J3, repeating that I owed $3,072,000, payable by credit link.

The next day, I phoned the Tannersville Library to talk to someone in circulation. The nice librarian smiled beautifully and told me, "Once we turn the matter over to J3, it's out of our hands. We don't handle our own long-term fines anymore."

Over the next ten days I tried everything I could think of. I called all the public officials in Tannersville; they all deferred to J3. I tried to find the human "handlers" of J3, and discovered it was controlled by a Texan debt collection agency, which wouldn't return my calls.

Finally a new message came in from J3, saying that if I did not begin paying the fine, it would start proceedings to garnish my bank account and wages.

I sat down heavily on my couch. If J3 garnished my wages at the statutory rate, it would take nearly 40 years to pay the fine. Bankruptcy? No, library fines were excluded from discharge under the new Act. I could try fighting it in court, but there was the fact that I'd knowingly taken out the book. I was pretty sure I could eventually prove that I owed only the fines on one book, but possibly not without a trial. Would they just wear me down with over-lawyering? I was willing to bet that the Texans, like collection agencies everywhere, would gladly pour motions and document requests over you until you drowned. Was there no way out?

I looked at the message again. I hadn't actually been served with notice of a lawsuit, and none of my assets had yet been attached. So far as I *actually* knew, there was no lawsuit and never would be. If I tried to flee the jurisdiction, they could still serve by publication. What if . . .

The next day I went to see Matthew Johnston at Catskill Features. His smile was as minty as ever, with a touch of baking soda.

"Would Catskill be willing to put me into Preservative Hibernation now?"

His eyes looked startled, but his smile didn't waver. "Are you ill?"

"No. I was thinking it would be nice to see the future."

"Well, I don't know. We've never had anyone *ask* to go into hibernation before. In fact, it's so new, I think we've had only a handful of our older writers and artists go in, from the Tuscon office." He looked at me sharply. "You do understand, don't you, that you would not continue to be paid during your hibernation? You're not an actual employee unless you're able to work."

"Sure, that was in the contract. But you'd still get the advantage of my copyright licenses, wouldn't you?"

"Yes, for a time, but the hibernation is meant to last only until we are able to cure you of your illness. How would we know when to revive you?"

"You could do it after a set number of years, and then I could go to work for you again."

"How long did you have in mind?"

I'd considered every time-based limitation on remedies I could think of. If I was right, then J3 couldn't serve me with papers, attach my assets or claim additional charges while I was hibernating. After long enough, the statute of limitations and other rules would prevent J3 from reopening a debt-collection matter. But I had to act quickly.

"Maybe thirty years?"

♎

The Preservative Hibernation vault looked like every bad movie about suspended animation you've ever seen, right down to the Snow-White style glass coffins and the wisps of water vapor swirling up from mysterious valves underneath. Actually it might have been dry ice; this was Catskill Features, Inc., and I wouldn't put it past them to throw in some cheap theatricality just for the hell of it. I could see that Johnston was right: there were only five or six chambers that were occupied (misted over on the inside, except for a clear area near the sleeper's face, just like in *2001: A Space Odyssey*). But the room contained perhaps fifty of these glitzy tombs, awaiting a freezerful of writers and artists, maintaining Catskill's control over intellectual property into eternity.

The technicians, naturally in white lab coats, looking like they'd all auditioned for the role of the Attractive Scientist, crowded around me as I came in. One asked me a long checklist of questions ("How long has it been since you've eaten?" "Have you had any sort of sexual encounter, including masturbation, in the last three hours?"). Another prepared the I.V. for the ichor or whatever that was going to keep my blood from freezing. A third wrapped my head in something that you could have used in the soon-to-be-released *Curse of the Mummy's Lawsuit.*

They had me sign six more consent forms. Naturally I read them all before signing, which made the Attractive Scientists purse their lips in impatience. But they were just the usual warnings about a hundred icky things that could go wrong, and the overbroad "indemnify and hold harmless" clause that purported to absolve Catskill from liability if its CEO murdered me in my sleep. Decent draftsmanship but not spectacular, meant more to discourage litigation than to change legal rights.

Finally I lay down in the chamber, suppressing an urge to cross my forearms over my chest like a Pharaoh. The cover came down in slow motion, and I could almost hear the brass-heavy orchestral score accompanying it. I felt a tingling in my left arm as the ichor began flowing in, followed by a sound like tinkling bells and fluffy clouds before my eyes. *Cheesy special effects* was my last thought before conking out.

♎

I woke up all of a sudden, to music coming out of tiny speakers in the coffin. It was "Constance's Friends," the theme song in the opening credits of every Catskill production and appearing in the most popular children's ride in the theme park. I opened my filmed-over eyes, then blinked to clear them. I inhaled deeply, feeling a crackle-crackle like bubble-wrap popping in my chest. Experimental wiggling of my fingers and toes confirmed that they stopped creaking like rusty hinges after a few seconds.

The lid came off the coffin with less ceremony than it had closed. I heard the echoes of a few dozen voices distributed around the vault; things were hopping. Standing over me was a thin, red-haired woman in a stained lab coat. Her name tag said *Cin.* She looked like she was under a lot of stress.

"Sit up," she said, not smiling.

I sat up like a piece of scenery being hoisted by lazy stagehands.

"Dizzy?" Cin asked.

I thought about it. "No."

"Good. Swing your legs over here."

I did so. "How long has it been?" I asked.

"Um," She frowned, checking her pad. "When did you go in?"

"February 28, 2107."

"Ten years."

"Not thirty?"

"Ten."

"But I thought my agreement — "

"What do you mean, 'agreement?' If you're going to die of a fatal illness, there's nothing I can do about that." Now her voice sounded bitter.

"No, no, I'm not. But I was supposed to be under for thirty years."

She found the paperwork she was looking for and flitted through it. "Yes, I see. Well, sorry. All of our hibernators are being thawed out today."

"Why?"

"Congress changed the Copyright Act, effective next month. Authors who go into hibernation don't get unlimited copyright anymore; it lasts for 90 years after publication only."

"So Catskill's license rights don't last any longer."

"Right. So there's no point spending a few million dollars a year keeping you people frozen."

There were groans and sobs from other corners of the room. "Look," Cin said. "Are you feeling okay? 'Cause if so, I need to be in about six other places. Here's the inventory of possessions you left with us when you went under, including your clothes. Head up to the eighteenth floor to get it all back." She looked me up and down. "Try standing up first."

I stood up. She stood with her arms folded, apparently waiting to see whether I would collapse. When I didn't, she nodded briefly and hurried across the vault.

♎

It turned out that the Copyright Act wasn't all that had changed. Over the last decade, thousands of people had used Preservative Hibernation as a way of tying up assets, avoiding taxation and keeping their wealth from their heirs. Tax law, banking law, estate law had had no provision for property owners in hibernation. These people put their money in to the hands of brokerage firms with power of attorney. Even with relatively low rates of return, the compounding of assets over time was impressive, and the firms managing the money got increasingly high, percentage-based fees. Increasing concentrations of wealth withdrew from the economy into the hands of people who were mostly asleep. Eventually heirs-at-law and devisees of wills got annoyed that they weren't getting any, and the tax authorities resented not having taxes to collect. So the law changed.

The weird thing is, I seem to have started it all. Okay, that's an exaggeration. But I was sort of the trigger.

Not that anybody knew who I was. But J3 apparently went to a lot of cybernetic effort to garnish my wages and my bank account, attach my other property, do whatever it could to get the fines paid, and failed every time as a result of my hibernation. The repeated failures made a lot of headlines. The court decisions all went against the debt collectors, and they were all publicized, blogged about, commented on, fought over. Nobody cared who *I* was; all that mattered was that J3 was unable to collect from a debtor because he was in hibernation and therefore unable to be served. When the statute of limitations ran, it made more headlines.

That's when people began thinking about the financial loopholes hibernation opened. I'd opened the original "loophole," but people found dozens of others. Then the backlash began and the system retaliated, not only in copyright, but laches, inheritance, securities, taxation, service of process, limitations, the works.

I didn't learn all of this immediately, of course. The first order of business was finding a place to live, and possibly some income. It wasn't clear whether Catskill would offer me my old job back; Constance the Cormorant was either having a mid-life crisis or undergoing celebrity rehab. In any case, the company had a full staff of writers, and I would need time to get up to speed.

But my saved salary had compounded nicely, and nobody had been able to touch it. I'd be able to live off it for a few years anyway, until I figured out how to make a living again. I found a new place and paid a cash security deposit, reconnected with the nets, and began exploring the job market for writers, writer-lawyers, lawyers, and unskilled laborers (because you never know).

Within a week, the following message appeared:

To: Eric Weiss
From: J5
Re: Library Fines
Date: June 15, 2117

Dear Mr. Weiss:

Your unpaid library fines, with interest, amount to $3,072,000. The interest and late-fees on these fines were tolled during the period February 28, 2107 – June 12, 2117. Interest will begin to accrue on this account as of June 12, 2117.

It is a pleasure doing business with you.

Yours very truly,

J5

J5, of course, turned out to be the latest model of J3, still owned and operated by the debt collection agency in Houston. But hadn't I escaped the library fines during the hibernation period? Hadn't the relevant statutes of limitations run?

I did some more research, and discovered a 2107 state statute, an amendment inserted into a bill on the inspection of garden tools five months after I went into hibernation. It provided a tolling of the statute of limitations for the payment of library fines if the debtor was in hibernation, and it was given retroactive application to February 28, 2017. The day I went into hibernation.

I called up the legislative history, and found that the lobbyist who had contacted Senator Borden to suggest the amendment worked for a fifth-level subsidiary of an innovative customer-service software unit. In other words, J3.

Given the money I now had in my account from my saved salary, I wondered whether it would now be worthwhile suing the Texans, or J5, to have the original debt declared invalid, or at least to have it reduced to the fine for one book, rather than thirty. But the statute of limitations for *that* action had expired during my hibernation, and there was no exception built in for it, since I went into hibernation after learning of the error.

But when I read J3's amendment in detail, I saw that it had an exception, similar to those I'd seen for other anti-hibernation statutes:

> Nothing in this Subsection shall apply to any debtor who enters preservative hibernation subsequent to contracting a fatal disease, as defined in Section 4(b), and who terminates hibernation when a cure for that disease is found.

A legislative compromise. Someone had objected to penalizing sick people for getting sick in order to get at financial scofflaws, so the sponsors of the bill inserted language exempting them.

So there was a way of escaping J5's clutches.

A little extreme, perhaps. . .

There was a quarantine for pneumonic plague patients at Washington Irving Memorial Hospital. Large warning signs shouted over each entrance to the affected ward, and there were annoyed staff members standing beneath them. But such precautions are designed to keep out the unwary and prevent the spread of infection, not to prevent inspections by skilled professionals.

I ostentatiously buttoned my lab coat and tied on my antiseptic mask while marching up to the nurse under the sign.

"Where's Masters?" I demanded.

"I'm sorry, who?"

"Masters, Lee Masters; he's supposed to meet me on this ward."

"I'm sorry, I don't think I know — "

I waved impatiently, looking at my watch and then my pad. "Look, I've got ten minutes before I've got to report. I'll do it without Masters if I have to."

"We're under quarantine — "

"Well, *obviously*," I said, pointing at my mask. "What do you want, a space suit?" Before she could answer, I squinted at the pad. "These are all headed for Preservative Hibernation?"

"Of course."

"How soon?"

"Later today."

"Which facility?"

"Nowlan."

"How many are there?"

"Twenty-two."

I nodded as if this confirmed what I'd thought, and took the sort of deep breath an impatient man takes when he's trying to calm himself down. "Okay, I'll only need to do a cursory survey; shouldn't take me more than ten minutes. If Masters gets here before I leave, please ask him to join me."

When I got into the ward, I made sure that there were no members of the hospital staff inside, then took off the mask. I went to each patient, half of whom were unconscious, and pretended to look into his or her eyes or feel their foreheads and necks, nodding with my best expression of sympathetic-yet-hopeful concern. I made a point of sniffing deeply near the patient's face, as if trying to detect an elusive smell for diagnostic purposes. Let me tell you, some of them smelled awful.

It had taken some out-of-my-field research to find the right bug. I needed an illness that was (1) fatal, (2) incurable, (3) easy to contract voluntarily, (4) quick to produce symptoms or lab results that would allow it to be diagnosed, with (5) a reasonable time-lag between diagnosis and irreversible damage. This eliminated 95% of the diseases that came to mind immediately — cancer, ebola, HIV, MS, ALS, influenza. I had hoped to find something blood-borne that I could inject myself with, but those blood and tissue samples were kept under tighter security than the contagious patients. I'd have had to learn burglary to get hold of them. This new, drug-resistant strain of pneumonic plague was much easier; it would turn symptomatic after two days and kill me in five, which was just about right.

I walked out of the ward wearing the surgical mask and kept it on for 48 hours to avoid becoming Typhoid Mary. Then, still wearing the mask, I went to a local clinic and reported the symptoms — fever, weakness, bloody cough, nausea — that had already begun to appear. Voila! I was in quarantine myself, and slated for Preservative Hibernation at the earliest opportunity.

Although Catskill wasn't about to hibernate me again, I contacted a commercial service; the clinic had several on its referral list, and would have sent me to a municipal facility if I hadn't been able to afford it. I decided to treat myself to a nice one.

Although feeling pretty woozy by this time, I was able to sign the seven or eight forms indicating that I was entering hibernation in order to prevent death from pneumonic plague. I sent copies, in envelopes I'd already prepared, to county courts, UCC filing agencies, banks, insurance companies and anyone else who might receive claims against me while I was under.

Contrasted to what I'd seen at Catskill, the hibernation room for Gilgamesh Preservation looked less like a vault and more like a luxury spa. The lab coats were tailored, multicolored and sexy, and you got your choice of music in the chamber, which felt like a cross between a tanning bed and a massage table. I kept expecting a floor show or vodka cocktails before the ichor kicked in and I went to sleep.

I got the vodka cocktail when they woke me. A beautiful young man named Pascal told me that I'd been asleep for 23 years, and that there was now a reliable serum to put pneumonic plague into permanent remission. A prescription had already been written by the Gilgamesh staff physician, and was waiting for me when I finished my cocktail.

So was a hardcopy letter:

November 21, 2140

Dear Mr. Weiss,

Congratulations on your recovery! You'll be happy to learn that, due to favorable changes in the interest compounding statutes, your fine is now only $76,466,558.00, which can be paid in cash or using any standard credit link.

We look forward to your prompt payment.

Best wishes,

J7

Once again, I had started a chain reaction. J5's failure to collect against me in 2117 in had resulted in a battalion of copycats, injecting themselves with all sorts of virulent diseases in order to take advantage of the statutory loopholes provided for the sick. Another army of facilitators, money managers, and annuity writers had made fortunes bigger than some city budgets by helping them along.

And once again, the loopholes had been closed by statute, exceptions created to exceptions, so that now the deliberate contraction of a fatal illness did not trigger any of the protections provided for in the earlier laws.

Of course, the earliest of these, related to library fines, was retroactive to 2117, and of course it had been instigated by J5.

I was ready to roll up my sleeves and begin looking for more gaps in the statutes, but when I reanimated my data account in the plush, wood-paneled room Gilgamesh kept for revived sleepers to catch up on their mail, among the thousands of junk messages I found an electronic statement from the Neighborhood Bank of Tannersville.

It took me a while to dredge up what connection I had with FNBT, but then it came to me: It was the custodial account in which I'd put my royalties from *Harriman's Loophole*, now more than forty years ago. I'd given the custodians considerable leeway, agreeing to a balance-percentage fee that paid them more as the size of the holdings increased. Their cut had been sliced down by the intervening statutes, but they'd achieved some remarkable success, reinvesting dividends and interest, making strategic sales and cashing in on temporary market fluctuations, and the balance, after taxes had been deducted was —

$76,466,583.58.

I stared at the number with my mouth open. The size of the balance was partially due to the tax exemptions and loopholes I'd created with my first hibernation.

I admit that I actually paused for a few minutes, drumming my fingers on the marble tabletop in iambic pentameter. A large and enthusiastic part of me wanted to outsmart J7 one more time, just to show I could do it. That love of competition and cleverness is the sort of thing that makes a lot of people stay in law practice.

But I *hadn't* stayed in law practice. I wanted, I reminded myself, to *create*, not just maneuver and evade. I hadn't done anything like creating since J3 started me on this game of fox and rabbit, and if I kept at it, I never would. I'd had my fun, I'd shown I could escape the trunk and handcuffs with the best of them. It was time to stop.

Slow as a child just learning to type, I keyed in the credit link transfer to J7. With the help of one of Pascal's friends, I got the remaining $25.58 in cash.

I walked out the front door of Gilgamesh, found a taxi, and told the driver to go north until the amount on the meter exactly matched $25.58. Then I got out and paid him.

He was unhappy that he didn't get a tip.

When I teach copyright law, I mention the Sonny Bono Copyright Extension Act, widely thought to have been the result of intense lobbying by the Walt Disney Company, which purportedly was trying to prevent Mickey Mouse from going into the public domain in 2017.

On one occasion a student asked me, "Didn't they freeze Walt Disney?" I answered, "Even if they had, he was already dead, so it wouldn't affect the copyright period." But then I thought, What if he hadn't already been dead?

This story was written as part of a Kickstarter project, and several characters have the tuckerized names of my backers. Other names are drawn from works of fiction with similar themes. Eric (Ehrich) Weiss is somebody else, of course.

— KLS

II

The Heart

Liza's Home

Liza can either help Ellie clean up the mess she's just made of her cereal or help Bess clean up the mess she's just made of herself. Her nose dictates the answer; grimly, she chooses Bess, taking the old woman by the arm and steering her towards the bathroom.

"Mooooooom!" complains Ellie from behind.

"Don't call me 'Mom'," says Liza to the girl. "Do the best you can; use the towels on the refrigerator handle. I'll be right back to help you when I'm done."

Bess allows herself to be led as if she were a calf on a rope. The set of her mouth betrays that she knows she's done something wrong but has too much dignity to say so. Liza helps Bess undress, gets her into the shower, uses the hand-held nozzle to clean her off, wraps her in a towel, discards the mess, throws the soiled clothes in the wash, quickly disinfects the shower, and finds something else for her to wear. Bess tolerates all of this without complaint or thanks, looking off in another direction.

By the time Liza returns to the kitchen, Ellie has finished cleaning up the cereal, using too many paper towels which are now piled up in the trash can, not the cloth towels Liza had in mind. Ellie's trying to make herself a sandwich for her lunch bag, tongue between her teeth, brow furrowed, uneven lumps of peanut butter interspersed with craters and rips on the bread. Liza can read the desperation; she moves in to take over.

"Thank you," says Ellie in a small voice.

"Good job, honey. Soon you'll get the hang of this." Liza smooths out the peanut butter, pastes together the severed bread.

"I was worried about the bus."

"I know you were. That was the right thing to do, making your sandwich for yourself; I'm proud of you." She flips the undamaged top piece onto the repaired lower half, tosses it into a plastic bag, and puts the whole thing into a paper bag with a hastily-washed apple. "I'm sorry I wasn't able to do it myself. I was taking care of Bess."

"You're always taking care of Bess," says Ellie, putting on her winter coat.

"Except when I'm taking care of you," says Liza, in what she intends to be a jocular tone, but isn't.

"It's not my fault," says Ellie, so quietly that Liza can barely hear.

"No, no, of course it's not," says Liza quickly, pulling Ellie into a fierce hug, feeling the zipper of Ellie's hood bite into her neck. "It's not your fault; it was never your fault. You know that, don't you?" In the back of her head, a voice says, *It's my fault; I did this to you.*

"Yes, I know," says Ellie in her ear. "I...." She stops, inhales twice. "I miss my real mom."

"I know, I know you do. I'm sorry. But you know I love you, right?"

Ellie pulls away from Liza and nods gravely. Then a muscle twitches near her ear. "The bus," she says.

"Off you go," says Liza, giving her a kiss on the cheek. Ellie only flinches a little. Inwardly Liza flinches too; it still feels vaguely indecent.

As the cold air from the door reaches into the house, Liza watches Ellie step into the bus with a mindfulness that's only dimly familiar. *When do we outgrow such things?*

Bess's wavering voice comes from behind her. "Lovely girl, that. What's her name again?"

"Ellie," says Liza for the twentieth time this week, turning to face her.

Bess perks up at that. "Yes?" she says expectantly. Slowly enunciating each word, Liza repeats, "The girl's name is Ellie."

The look on Bess's face is as delighted as if she has just witnessed a magic trick. "Ellie!" She laughs. "Ellie! Fancy that!"

Then she squints at Liza.

"And what's your name, dear? I'm sorry, it just keeps slipping my mind." Bess's voice is sociable, light, but her eyes are terrified.

"Liza," says Liza, for the third time this morning.

Her name sparks no recognition.

♎

Mark warned her; he told her to wait.

The tiny, overly-bright project office they shared in the engineering lab didn't give room to pace, so he fidgeted instead, grabbing staple removers and rulers and dropping them again. In a tight voice, he said, "The displacement equations don't resolve in the return direction." His tone was halfway between lecturing and pleading; he picked up a pencil and gripped it tightly in both hands.

"You might wind up somewhere you don't speak the language, a hundred years too early. And what if you change the past, what if you're not here in that other future? What if you erase yourself? Or what if there are two of you, one who remembers and one who doesn't? What'll you do then?"

Liza flicked her hand dismissively. "What if a white rabbit pulls a pocket watch from his waistcoat and tells me he's late?"

"Liza — "

"Well, it's all speculation, isn't it? You're making up every disaster that could happen, just to talk me out of it."

"You know that's — These are real-world permutations of some of the solutions to the equations; there are half a dozen others. There's even the possibility of *bounce*: the cycle repeats, sends you God knows where, then brings you back here. Or maybe it doesn't bring you back at all."

The pencil in his hands snapped. He threw it at the wastebasket. Liza stared at it, willing the two pieces to come back together and form a whole. They stayed broken.

He continued, "You need to be patient. We won't stop working on the displacer. As the data comes in, we'll eliminate solutions. In five, ten years, I'm sure we'll be able to drop you exactly where you need to be, in the right time and place, and yank you back without a hitch. But if you displace before we've solved those problems, if I lose you, then I'll be working on it alone, and I'll probably never get it right. You'll be stranded for good. Why take the risk now?"

She hugged herself as if she were cold. "Because my mother died at fifty-two and my father at fifty-eight. I don't know that I *have* ten years, Mark."

They argued past two in the morning, getting nowhere. Mark's resistance was more than professional, and it touched her. But for Liza, the whole point of the displacer, the justification for engendering it, giving birth to it, enslaving her adulthood to it, was the chance to cheat fate, to prevent the inevitable, to repair injustice.

Eventually Liza gave in, or at least pretended to. Mark could not understand the unscientific, untechnical urgency she felt.

Not too long after that, he had dinner at her apartment, the only time ever. He had been trying, in his tentative, roundabout way, to nudge her into a romance, and she invited him, though she couldn't cook worth a damn and usually avoided company. When she thought about it, her disinclination puzzled Liza herself. Why not have a companion? Why be alone?

When he entered the apartment, he stood for a moment in the doorway, the light from the common hall streaming in behind him. His eyes widened in a friendly, nervous way, and Liza realized that he thought the lowered lighting was meant to create a romantic mood.

"I always keep the lights down and the heat up," she said. Does it bother you?"

"No, not if you don't mind my taking off my sweater. Otherwise I'll boil."

Boiling was pretty much what she was doing by way of preparing dinner, and she nodded quickly and went back to the kitchen to see to the pots. When she returned, he was in his cream-colored shirt, sleeves rolled up past the elbows, staring at the photos on the wall.

"These are all the same girl," he said. "You?"

"No, that's Dinah."

She said nothing more. Mark reached over as if to adjust the frame of one of the pictures, but stopped at Liza's quick little intake of breath. She smiled apologetically, ashamed.

He ventured again, "Your niece?"

She shook her head. "She died when she was eight. An accident. More than forty years, now."

"I'm sorry." He waited, but she said nothing more, going back into the kitchen, coming out with pasta and a sauce that she'd heated up from a package.

Mark found nice things to say about the dinner, and tried to talk about other things too, but his voice kept trailing off as he was distracted by the shrine on the walls. For her part, Liza was wondering how she felt about this man sitting across from her, trying to imagine what it would be like to have him in that chair every morning.

Eventually he frowned at her, knitting his brow as if trying to think of how to phrase something. Then he said, "Forty years is a long time."

"I suppose."

"Most people — I don't think most people would have so many pictures, not after so long." His voice was neutral, but she could feel his probing, like when he was running a circuit test in the lab.

"I guess."

"Do you — do you know why you've got so many photos of Dinah, and none of anybody else?"

Liza felt tension in her jaw, but tried to relax. She knew he was trying to avoid saying it wasn't normal to have a gallery devoted to a girl long dead. Liza would have liked to be able to explain herself to him, but some angry part of her mind snapped that it was natural, it was normal, who wouldn't, to keep Dinah's memory alive? Who wouldn't think of her every day? Who wouldn't try to save her life?

In that instant of clarity, she realized that, feelings for him or no, she'd have slept with Mark, if necessary, so she could keep working on the displacer. It was a wild, weird thought; the project was easily as much hers as his, maybe more, and Mark was not the sort even to imagine such a *quid pro quo*. Where had that idea come from?

Dinner ended, and they made pleasant noises about doing it again.

Ω

Before sunrise, Liza dressed in vintage clothes from thrift shops, pocketed old money she'd been saving for years, and made her way to the lab while Mark was probably still alone in his bed.

The morning rays were just beginning to push through the brilliant red-and-orange leaves as she entered the project room. She'd already completed the calculations, but she checked them again, adjusting frequencies and field focus. Her touch was light and soothing over the pathways and controls, the only children she would ever have. Saying the closest thing to a prayer she'd uttered since her own childhood, she began the sequence.

Every sense overloaded. Searing light ripped through her closed lids, shrieking chords tore at her ears, bitter metallic saliva engulfed her tongue, and her nostrils reeked with the stench of putrefaction. Worst, her spine felt like it was being burned from the inside with acid. Had she been able to move, she would have screamed.

As quickly as it had started, it stopped. Liza stumbled and nearly fell into a brick wall, cool against the suddenly-hot air, dark compared to the brightness in front of her. She could not tell how long the torture had lasted; 'how long' was probably a meaningless question anyway.

She was on the sidewalk in front of a shopping center, facing a parking lot washed out with summer sun; heat waves jiggled the cars, which were longer, more stately than the cars she knew. More of them were on the busy boulevard beyond the parking lot.

Her heart pounded; she recognized that street. And, yes, although she was against a wall, in the shade, she felt the oppressive steaminess of a southeast-Michigan summer.

A glass door opened three yards to her right and a whisper of drier air reached her, carrying a hint of popcorn and newly-sized fabric. She knew that smell, though she'd forgotten it. She was outside the K-mart at Beech and Eight Mile, less than two miles from where she needed to go. *Bullseye, Mark!*

How about the temporal displacement? Nearby, she found a newspaper vendor, fished out the right coins, and looked at the date at the top of the paper:

Tuesday, July 25, 1967

"Perfect, perfect!" *Down to the very day! Down to the—* She needed to find a clock.

Inside the K-mart, the wall clock said it was half-past twelve. Later than she'd planned, but early enough, just barely. If she waited for a bus (and now she remembered there were few buses in this part of Detroit in 1967), she'd be too late. She went to the corner, crossed Beech Road and turned right, and began to walk.

The heat moved around her like a living thing as she followed the road down to the bridge and up the next hill; drugged bees drifted and dipped around her. Close as she was to the border of Detroit itself, in this era things turned rural pretty fast. The road was dirt and gravel, coated in oil once a year to keep the dust down; she'd remembered it wasn't paved, but had forgotten the oil. Now the thick, tarry smell called up memories of complicated rainbows in little puddles after a summer shower. But it was difficult, walking on a gravel road in shoes like hers; try as she might, she couldn't avoid all the slippery rocks, and she twisted her left ankle on the way up the hill.

As she continued north, limping slightly, a hearse passed her on the right, followed by a procession of slow-moving cars with little flags. Not so soon, surely? Was she too late already? But no, this was only the first of the corteges. There would be four that day, all heading to the Catholic cemetery at the end of the road. Four funerals in one day would be unusual for that cemetery, but not in July of 1967.

She still had time.

When she reached the Marathon station at the top of the hill, she bought a Coke from a vending machine, mopping her brow. Her blouse was sticking to her and her neck was coated with sweat. The clock in the station said it was nearly one in the afternoon; it would be happening soon. She had to keep on.

She crossed Nine Mile Road, noticing the lack of a traffic light and trying to recall when they'd installed it. There was nothing on this corner now except the gas station; down the street she could just make out the junior high school, still new.

Another half mile, just after the second hearse overtook her, and she saw the house: a tan-brick ranch on a sleepy side street, sporting a circular drive that reached both Beech and the side street. Dutch elms flanked the driveway, and playing under one of them were two little girls, aged eight and seven.

Two. Dinah and Ellie.

Ellie was there.

Now that she saw her, it was obvious to Liza that Ellie would be, should be, there at this moment. But why hadn't she remembered? What did she think she remembered instead?

All her plans had involved Dinah, what to do about Dinah; no thought of Ellie had ever crossed her mind. She wanted to take Dinah in her arms and shield her, but watching Ellie's serious, lively face, Liza felt nauseous. It made sense, and it didn't make sense, and something was keeping the pieces from fitting.

The girls hadn't seen her yet. She hung back, moving behind one of the old apple trees that still decorated the neighborhood. Her foot slipped on a green apple rotting on the neighbors' lawn, and she twisted the same ankle again. She bit her lip so as not to cry out.

Her plan had been to convince Dinah to go inside before the fourth cortege came along. All right, she'd get both of them to go. They were pointing at the second procession as it passed. Yesterday, Liza knew, they'd also seen a series of solemn cars and little flags; they were speculating, little-girl fashion, as to how long it would be before the next one.

If she was to persuade both girls at once, she would need more time. On the other hand, if she arrived too early, they'd have time to talk to their mother and come back outside. Maybe the arrival of a strange adult would send them screeching into the house for their mother anyway? Probably not; they'd both be curious, especially Ellie.

Ellie. Ellie was here.

The third cortege arrived. Liza stepped out from behind the apple tree, limping more than ever, and crossed towards the girls under the elm.

They were playing a game now: Who can pick up the darkest of the oil-covered rocks from the road and run back to the tree with it before the next car comes? Ellie, the younger, was taunting Dinah. "You're so *slow!* I'm gonna win!"

You're so slow. You're so slow. Images, sounds, poured into Liza's head like water from a burst balloon. She nearly fell over with vertigo.

You're so slow. Ellie, teasing Dinah. Dinah, so angry, so easily provoked by her little sister. *You're so slow*. Dinah staying on the road longer, longer, Ellie jeering, "You're so slow!" Then there would be the blowout, the car swerving, sliding out of the cortege —

Ellie's fault. It *was* Ellie's fault. Liza stood transfixed, unable to move.

The girls saw her. "Who are you?" Ellie called.

"Liza," Liza grunted, not really focusing, not knowing what to do. The third cortege finished passing.

"Dinah," she said, trying to get control of her voice. "Go inside and see your mother. You too, Ellie."

"Why?" demanded Ellie as Dinah obediently started to rise.

"Do as I say," said Liza, a harsh sound coming from her throat. Dinah ran into the house.

"You're not my mother," said Ellie. "I don't have to do what you say."

Liza could hear the last cortege coming up the road. "Ellie, *go in*."

"How do you know my name?" asked Ellie. "I don't know you."

"There's no time," said Liza. The car would slide all the way to the elm tree; Ellie now stood directly in its path.

Desperate, she tried again. "Ellie, come here, come around the tree! It's important!"

Ellie stood indecisively. Liza ran over, grabbed Ellie, and pulled her away from the tree, just as she heard the tire explode like a pistol shot. Ellie screamed. The oversized blue sedan slid on the oily gravel and spun into the elm with a smashing, tearing sound, missing them by only a yard, and the tree snapped and began to fall. Ellie screamed again, clutching frantically at Liza.

Liza put her arms around the girl, trying to speak softly, but her own voice was shaking too much —

Then she felt the agony down the center of her spine, saw the blinding light, smelled the reek. She couldn't feel anything but the pain, couldn't hear anything but the awful chords, but she knew Ellie was still clutching her, screaming into eternity.

When it stopped, the girl whimpered and clung to the woman, hiding her face in Liza's blouse.

They hadn't moved. They were still on the lawn of the house. But the elm tree was straight and undamaged; the bushes around them had a thousand pink-and-white spring flowers. The breeze was warm, not hot, and thick with scent.

Two little girls played on a swing set, a four-year-old and a five-year-old. Their mother was close by.

Ellie and Dinah.

"The cycle repeats," Liza croaked.

They had come backwards three years, to before the accident had happened, would happen. A displacement echo, just as Mark had feared.

At the sound of Liza's words, the girls' mother looked up. Ellie, the Ellie who was with Liza, shrieked, "*Mommy!*"

Liza dug her fingers into the girl's shoulder, not letting her go. At the same moment, startled by the sudden yell, the other Ellie, the Ellie on the swing, fell off. Her leg bent sharply at the wrong angle; Liza imagined she could hear the *snap*. The smaller Ellie cried out. The larger Ellie screamed.

And it all vanished: swing, mother, Dinah, Ellie with a broken leg. In their place were torment and madness in her eyes and ears, as if she'd never experienced anything else.

Then the pain stopped again, and did not return. Liza and Ellie shivered in sudden cold.

It seemed to be late fall, with an unforgiving wind under a weak gray sky that barely lit the unfamiliar street and buildings around them. She stared at the cars on the street; they were smaller, quieter than any she'd ever seen, traveling on narrow roads full of pedestrians in strange clothes.

This wasn't where she'd started.

"Where are we?" whimpered Ellie. Liza put her arm around the girl to keep her warm, but Ellie pulled away, staring at Liza as if she were a ghost.

They walked, Liza limping, until they happened upon an electronic kiosk with the date, time, and weather flashing on it:

Sat 20 Nov 2049

14:23

Cloudy 10° C

"Take me home," said Ellie, then started to cry. "Please take me home."

The date flashed over and over, as if to remind Liza of her folly.

Mark had been right. A final forward differential of exactly twice the initial jump, which told Liza which of the multiple solutions to the equations was the right one. He'd be happy to know.

She found him, finally, in a twenty-year-old obituary in the local public library database; he had succumbed to an epidemic, unmarried, leaving no family. Alone.

She could find no record of the displacer — no published papers, no news articles, no correspondence. Perhaps it had never existed in this timeline, or perhaps Mark never resumed work on it after she abused the technology. Liza probably could rebuild the displacer if she had access to funding, if she could get the support of a lab, if she were someone anyone could trust. But what was she to say, that she was an engineer recently arrived from 2008, courtesy of her own time machine? She'd be lucky not to find herself locked up and drugged. And what would happen to Ellie?

In the eighty-two years since the fourth cortege, the two of them had outlived everyone who might have known Liza, everyone who'd ever heard of Ellie. They looked for Dinah, but she'd died of cancer in 2010. *Forty-three extra years,* Liza told herself, tried to tell herself. *I gave her forty-three extra years, even if I'll never see her.*

Collectors bought her vintage money at a premium, but the proceeds still ran out quickly. They were exiles, alone and without succor — until Bess.

They found Bess almost by accident. Liza didn't really believe the address listing when she saw it, and they visited the little house, spending their last few dollars, more out of dogged desperation than hope. But there Bess was — falling apart, nearly helpless, her dwelling a foul-smelling, chaotic wreck — a crazy old woman who should not, could not, be there at all.

Liza asked Bess about her past, trying to reconstruct how she came to be in this place, in this time. Bess's memory was already so mangled that Liza got nothing but vague allusions to people and places she didn't recognize — except for the occasional calm, chilling reference to Dinah. When Liza tried to follow up on those tantalizing hints, the responses only left her confused.

Yet Bess recognized something: she seemed to know Ellie and repeatedly asked where they'd met. Not Liza; Liza was a stranger.

Nonetheless, here was a place of refuge, the only place to which Liza or Ellie had any claim. And Bess had a claim on them too: having seen the squalor and filth in which she lived, Liza found it impossible to turn away. Quickly and quietly they moved in with her, the woman and the girl, and Liza, who'd never taken care of anyone, found herself looking after a child and an increasingly incompetent nonagenarian at once.

Even with technical skills as badly outdated as hers, some rapid self-education qualified Liza for work checking designs for performance parameters and component tolerances. It didn't pay much, but she could do it from home — for this was home, now, and she was needed. Bess could not be trusted on her own; Ellie, now enrolled in a school on the strength of partially-forged identity papers, needed to return from each bewildering day to a home, a family.

Except that they weren't a family.

♎

Liza is preparing a tuna casserole. Bess and Ellie are sitting at a rickety card table, playing checkers. It's something they have in common, and Ellie's impetuousness and inexperience are matched by Bess's wandering mind. Neither of them wants Liza's help in the game, and neither wants to play it with her.

It's a cold winter evening, the sky already dark; the warmth of the kitchen before dinner makes them grateful.

Bess gazes at Ellie over the chessboard. "What's your name?" she asks. "You look familiar."

Ellie keeps her face steady. Liza's proud of her; it isn't easy for an eight-year-old to hear the same question asked over and over and not react.

"I'm Ellie," says Ellie. "Short for Elizabeth."

Bess's eyes widen in wonder. "So am I! I'm Ellie!"

Ellie takes a breath before answering. "No, you're Bess. Bess is short for Elizabeth too."

"Elizabeth! What a coincidence! That's my name."

"I know," says Ellie, her eyes closing briefly.

"And what's her name?" Bess asks in a conspiratorial whisper, as if Liza can't hear her.

Ellie's lip trembles. "Liza. That's — " But she cannot finish the sentence.

Bess laughs and claps her hands, as if this is the best joke she's ever heard.

Liza has tracked down documents and pieced much of the older woman's history together. Sometime, somewhere, when this Elizabeth Hanover outgrew Ellie, she became Bess instead of Liza.

Ellie is familiar; Ellie is Elizabeth as Bess remembers herself.

But Liza has come to understand that Bess's history has been far different than Liza's own. No research into relativistic displacement, no obsessive drive towards a technology of meddling and redemption. Without Dinah's death as a spur, Bess ended up teaching French at the local community college, performing competently and unremarkably for nearly fifty years. No wonder she doesn't recognize Liza.

But in this they are alike: Bess has always been alone.

If any fellow teacher ever approached her in the same shy way that Mark approached Liza, nothing came of it. The only greeting cards or keepsakes Bess has are Dinah's, and only two or three of those.

Liza goes back to making the tuna casserole. She doesn't much care for it herself, not anymore, but it's comforting to Ellie, and of course Liza knows how to make it exactly as her mother did. Comfort food for Liza, now, would be sushi or tapas, foods she ate in college or with colleagues like Mark, foods that neither Bess nor Ellie enjoys. Bess likes the tuna casserole as Ellie does.

On her shoulder, Liza feels Bess's hand, with the arthritic bulges in the joints of the thumb and forefinger. She turns around to see the labyrinthine, age-scarred face, the face she can't bear to look at, the face that will one day stare at her out of a mirror.

"You can't help where I'm going," says Bess, grasping Liza's shoulder so hard it hurts.

"What?"

"You can't help where you're going either." It's singsong, like a nursery rhyme.

"I don't understand." She needs to get the casserole in the oven.

"You can't help where she's going either," says Bess, gesturing at Ellie.

Liza's frightened now. Nonsense. Crazy, crazy old woman.

"Elizabeth, Elizabeth, Elizabeth," sings Bess. "Elizabeth's going to die. Three times." She laughs.

"I know." Liza's trembling, unable to keep the casserole steady. She lets it clunk down on the counter.

"You can't help any of it."

"I *know!*" Now Liza is crying. Bess takes her into a spindly, motherly hug.

"Hush now," she says, in the same lullaby voice.

Liza begins to sob outright, speaking in gasps. "I'm so stupid. It's all my fault."

"Yes, it is," says Bess agreeably.

"I took her mother. I took everything."

"You," says Bess, pulling away and smiling. "You're her mother."

"Not. Nobody's mother."

Liza releases herself to her tears, allowing Bess to pat her. After a few minutes she feels Ellie's arms round her stomach from behind, Ellie's head against her back.

"It's okay, Liza," says Ellie's voice, vibrating in her belly. "It's okay. I'll be okay."

"You — " Liza hiccups, tries again. "You can call me 'Mom' if you want to."

"Okay," says Ellie, her voice trembling. Then she gives Liza one last squeeze, takes Bess's hand, and leads her back to the checkerboard.

My sister once described herself as a "boglona mom", sandwiched between caring for our mother and caring for her own young children. That made me think about how caring for others is often a metaphor for care of the self; we're imagining how we would want to be cared for. Then, like a science fiction writer, I wondered about making the metaphor literal.

Naturally that was going to be a time travel story, and one that owed a big-time debt to David Gerrold's The Man Who Folded Himself *and Robert Heinlein's " 'All You Zombies — ' ". When we think about changing the past, we're really thinking about changing ourselves, which makes it all the worse when we inevitably fail.*

Ellie and Dinah's house is the one I grew up in. I can remember the smell of that K-mart and the oily gravel on that road as if it were last week.

— KLS

The Orpheus Fountain

Vic and Clara had their heads together, examining the scans of Laura Teng's brain. Through the years they had learned to do this without any public display of affection, although colleagues still teased them about it. "There go Doctor and Doctor Swensen again," they would say. "There are empty beds down the corridor, you know." It was touching, really, after all this time.

Vic glanced at Clara; from this angle he could see only her tight, dark curls with their silver gilding and the tip of her slender nose, but he knew that she wanted to speak first.

"Normal," she said. "Nice, normal and boring."

"Seems so," said Vic.

From behind them, Fergus said, "Good. That means there are no impediments to the procedure."

Clara turned around to look at Fergus, unconsciously rubbing the cuff of her lab coat between her fingers. "No reason for it, either."

"Clara — " began Fergus.

"There is nothing wrong with that brain. No damage at all."

"Except that she can't remember anything that happened during the last five years," said Vic.

"That's my point," said Clara. She released her cuff and started counting on her fingers. "Can't remember events, doesn't recognize people she met, has even lost skills she learned. This isn't declarative memory loss; it's functional memory loss."

"Right," said Vic.

"So it's not the result of anything organic. It's psychogenic. She needs therapy, not rewiring."

Fergus sighed. "You've seen the preliminary trial results. You know what I'm trying to do."

Clara looked sour. "Have you spoken with Melissa?"

"The psychiatrist? Yes; she thinks it might help."

"Well then, you don't really need to consult us, do you?"

"Clara," said Vic.

Fergus asked, "Will you present it to the patient as an option?"

"Of course," said Clara.

"Objectively?"

"Now, *look*," said Vic, beginning to step towards Fergus before Clara touched his arm. He stopped, glanced toward her, looked back at Fergus. "That was out of line," he said.

"Yes, you're right," said Fergus. "I apologize, Clara."

"You bet you do," said Vic.

"Vic." Clara said. "It's all right, Fergus."

Later in the bright, noisy corridor, Clara punched Vic lightly in the arm. "You," she said. "He's ten years younger than you are."

He punched her in the arm too. "Embarrassed?"

"No, nostalgic. I remember when you were a hothead like that all the time, always charging off into battle for your Lady Fair."

"Mm, Lady Dark, I think. It's sublimation: got stuck in neurology instead of becoming a superhero or an oncologist. Anyway, my lady never let me get into a real battle."

"Your lady had better uses for you. You regret the neurology?"

He smiled. "Nope. Have a good lab partner."

They turned a corner. Vic motioned in the direction of the cafeteria with his head; Clara made a face and mouthed the word *home*.

"I'll ask Tina to set up an appointment with Laura this week, so that we can discuss Fergus's procedure," said Vic. When Clara didn't answer, he added, "It might help."

"Fergus doesn't care about whether it helps. He cares about winning a stupid Nobel Prize."

"Well, he stands a better chance of winning it if it does help, right?" Clara responded with a hand gesture that meant, *whatever*. "Wouldn't mind getting one of those prizes myself, if I were doing that kind of work."

"Sure," said Clara. "It would look perfect next to your fraternity picture."

He snorted. "Or maybe under the Orpheus Fountain in the bedroom."

She imitated his snort, a half-octave higher. "Yes, that could work, but only if I sleep in the guest room."

The Orpheus Fountain exists in two places at once, but one of them is incomplete. The sculptor Carl Milles nestled the original in the Market Square of his beloved Stockholm. Orpheus, godlike in size, suspended above earth as if by magic, plays the piteous chord at his moment of realization that Eurydice is lost to him forever. Beneath him in a circle, smaller than Orpheus but still larger than life, are eight listeners, roused from the dead or from the future by the despair of his music. They have looked up suddenly, frozen in whatever they were doing, unable to turn away, and unable, after this moment, to be free of the echo of Orpheus's pain. One of these, clearly Ludwig van Beethoven, holds his hands before his face with his eyes shut, lost in rapture and agony.

Milles raised the other fountain on the campus of one of the schools at Cranbrook, his adopted home in the United States. It is identical to the sculpture in Stockholm, except for this: Orpheus himself is missing. The eight listeners turn their heads towards the empty center of their circle. The viewer does not know where the music comes from, does not know the source of Beethoven's awful ecstasy.

Clara finished her last bit of pasta, then skewered the one on Vic's plate that he wasn't going to eat. Vic put down his glass of wine, reached across the table and slowly ran his finger down the inside of Clara's forearm. She looked up at him; he raised his eyebrows.

"Dishes," she said.

He snorted, knowing it would make her scowl, as they rose with plates in their hands.

But after they had cleared the dishes, as Vic was trying to maneuver past Clara to get to the dishwasher, she turned completely around and hooked her arms behind his neck, although he was still holding the saucepan. He hated it when she jumped him while he was holding things, but she melted against him and melted their mouths together, her eyes shut. He put his free hand around her waist and tried to find someplace to set down the pan.

Upstairs, they undressed before getting into bed; Clara hung her blouse up for tomorrow and put her bra in the hand-wash basket. He noticed that she waited before removing her panties, because she knew he loved seeing the moment when they came off. When the blankets were up around their shoulders, she threw her leg casually over his hip. Their kisses were unhurried, amused, as they lazily moved against each other with conversational moans.

In almost the same motion, he pushed her onto her back and she pushed his head towards the foot of the bed, reaching for a pillow to put under her hips. Teasing and savoring Clara was like rereading a favorite book, like trying silly variations on a tune he knew by heart. About when he expected, she grabbed his hair with one hand, and he moved his own hand to answer what she didn't need to ask.

He kept his mind from wandering by softly telling her a favorite story while he touched her, timing it to the rhythm of her breathing, the pitch of her voice. When finally she sang the wordless, tuneless song that was the most beautiful sound in his world, he eased on top, and she clamped her legs around his back to pull him down. Vic moved slowly, wanting to prolong the sweet expectation, while Clara worked herself up to another song, panting into his ear. Then he could no longer contain himself, and experienced the moment that left him no less incredulous for all its familiarity.

For a calm, languid interval they lay together, and she played with his hair.

Eventually she reached down and pushed at his stomach, and he reached over to the bedside table and pulled out a bunch of tissues, giving some to her and using some himself.

They lay in bed reading, although Vic's eyelids were heavy almost immediately. The last thing he saw before switching off his light was the photo on the wall opposite the bed: the Orpheus Fountain.

♎

Vic spent his teenage school years at Cranbrook, passing the incomplete Orpheus Fountain practically every day between classes. A dozen times he stopped and looked at it, smiling at the water of the fountain, delighting in the bodies of the female figures, or wondering at the terrible knowledge in the faces. And although he'd been told that they were listening to Orpheus, he'd never known that there was another sculpture, never known that somewhere, Orpheus lived.

On their honeymoon Vic and Clara traveled for three weeks in Scandinavia, climbing fjords and swimming nude on the ephemeral summer beaches. They crossed the Arctic Circle in Lapland, marveling at a sun that circled without setting and a wasted landscape that seemed as alien as the Moon. Near the end of their trip they made love in a sumptuous hotel bed in Stockholm, and very late in the morning set out to explore. The Market Square had dozens of stalls, with cloudberries and other wonders. For them the world was just beginning, and everything seemed fresh and portentous. After laughing at Clara's purchase of more berries than they could possibly eat, Vic looked up for the first time.

It shook Clara to turn around and see the tears running down Vic's cheeks. He cried openly, grasping her hands as he gazed up at the tortured face of Orpheus, only now understanding why the fountain of his youth held so much pain. In broken words he told her, and she felt that he had opened a door for her that no one else would ever enter.

For their first anniversary, drinking the last of the leftover wedding champagne, Clara gave Vic a framed photograph of the Orpheus Fountain in Stockholm. On the back of the photo she had written, although he did not see it, *You will never lose me*. Since that day, the photograph graced every bedroom they shared.

♎

Sitting in Vic and Clara's consultation office, Laura Teng looked thin and fragile, although she was perfectly fit in all ways but one. Her nimble hands, which had been folded in her lap, now moved in an eloquent gesture of helplessness.

"I've counted thirty-five paintings I completed during those five years; I've read reviews of them; I've stared at them. The earlier ones I understand, but — " She shook her head. "The later ones might have been painted by a stranger. I can't see how I got to them. I don't know who I am, and I can't work. I feel frozen."

Vic picked up a file and took a breath to speak, but Clara shifted her weight to the other hip, so he waited.

Clara said, "Laura, usually the global sort of loss you are experiencing, that takes skills, faces and feelings from the same period as the memories of events, is caused by an emotional trauma. It might be something early, from childhood, or something more recent, say, near the beginning of the time when the memories vanish."

Laura nodded glumly, her hands twisting in her lap. "Melissa told me. She said that with therapy you can sometimes find the trauma and get back the memories. But she also said that a lot of people never get there at all. They never get back what they lost, no matter how much they want it."

Clara looked like she was about to say more, but stopped herself. Vic stepped into the pause. Clara tightened her lips as he spoke.

"There is another treatment we were going to offer you. It's experimental, but it may have some impact."

Laura had been disappointed many times; nonetheless Vic saw a hopeful look come into her eyes. "Really? What is it?"

"Researchers have catalogued a recognizable pattern of impulses, along particular collections of neurons, when someone is trying to recover a memory. It's unique and consistent for the same person looking for the same memory, even when she can't locate the memories. What's been noticed in cases like yours is that this pattern is missing when the patient tries to recover the memories in the 'lost' zone or period. It's as if some part of the brain isn't really trying."

Laura closed her eyes. "Like she doesn't really want to know." Clara nodded vigorously.

Vic continued. "Our colleague Fergus Catherwood has developed a process that simulates the memory-recovery pattern for a particular patient. He traces the recurrent retrieval patterns in that patient, then programs virus-sized stimulators that are injected and reside near the appropriate neurons. When the patient is directed to remember things from the lost period, the devices activate in sequence, giving the brain the signals it is accustomed to generate when memories actually are being sought. There's no reason the memories shouldn't still be in there somewhere, and in some cases the impulse pattern seems to trigger retrieval."

Clara cut in. "The work in this area is very new, and the clinical results so far have been mixed. It's promising, but far from certain. And although the treatment is 'safe' within normal experimental limits, there are risks. There could be some loss of motor or sensory function; there could be more memory loss."

Laura opened her eyes again. "How much more?"

Vic said, "We're not sure. It's a very low-incidence side effect, and typically the losses are small."

Clara said, "But we can't guarantee that. Therapy alone may be the safer way to go."

Laura studied Vic and Clara's diplomas on the wall, as if thinking how to compose a painting around them. Vic said, "If you're interested, we can put you in touch with Dr. Catherwood, and he can tell you more."

Then she slowly nodded her head three times, as if to the rhythm of a song. "I'll do it."

"You'll talk to him?"

"I'll have the procedure."

In the corridor, Clara unconsciously played with the pocket of her lab coat, the way she did when she was troubled. It made Vic smile.

"That young woman has massive talent and a good life. Experimental treatments..." Clara trailed off, worrying a thread.

"She wants what she had before," said Vic. "You can understand that."

"The past is over, Vic. The future's what matters."

♎

As Clara later remembered it, she was worried from the start about the tiny room Fergus was using for the injection of the stimulator units. She even remembered wondering why there were no restraints on the couch, although there was no reason Laura should have needed them. But perhaps Clara never had such thoughts; in hindsight our judgment is always better.

The plan was to introduce the units in suspension intravenously, then wheel the patient into Radiology to check whether the units had deployed themselves in the right locations and were firing properly.

Clara, Vic, and Fergus were all cramped into the room with Laura, although only Fergus himself was really necessary, and, indeed, for a straightforward matter like this, a nurse or P.A. would have sufficed. But Fergus always oversaw his own procedures, Vic was curious, and Clara felt responsible for Laura's taking this step.

Fergus had just added the vial containing the suspension to the saline feed and moved aside to make a note, when Laura's seizures began.

She had no history of any condition that should have caused seizures, nor should either the I.V. or the injected devices have triggered them. Melissa later hypothesized that whatever part of Laura was hiding from her memories was making a last-ditch effort to prevent them from being forced on her, but it was only a guess.

Everyone's first thought was to get any breakables away from Laura. The first throes ripped out the IV; Clara moved to pull it aside, especially the needle, but Vic was marginally closer to the couch and had that protective-lion look in his eye. He moved in first and grabbed the needle just as Laura's arm struck out.

Clara knew, from the way Vic's back stiffened, that he'd been hurt. Fergus, on the other side of the couch, involuntarily reached across the patient toward Vic, then stopped himself. Vic backed away from Laura, pulling the I.V. assembly with him and yanking the needle out of his own hand in the same motion.

He looked down at his hand, annoyed, then up at Clara, sheepish. Then he frowned and tilted his head, as if he were listening to distant music, as his mind was invaded by ten or twenty thousand tiny machines programmed to sculpt the workings of somebody else's brain.

As Laura's seizures subsided, Vic toppled over so silently that Clara wondered whether she had gone deaf.

Clara strode into the hospital, waving at the staff and smiling as if this were any ordinary day at work. She fooled no one: they all knew that this was the day that Vic was getting out of Rehab, but out of kindness they did not notice her anxiety.

She went up to his room, which was made up for the next patient. Vic was already packed, sitting on the chair next to the bed, reading a magazine. He looked up and smiled when she came in.

"Hi, Clara," he said.

"Hello there."

There was a pause.

"Go ahead," he said quietly. "You can ask me."

She took a breath and said, "How much do you remember?"

Matter-of-factly, as if it caused him no pain, he answered, "Nothing between the day of my college graduation and the day I woke up in the hospital. Basically the same as before."

She nodded in what she tried to make look like a nonchalant manner, fiddling with his suitcase. His entire career, medical school, twenty-two years of his life — and her. Not a scrap of their courtship, their marriage, their partnership, nothing. She was a middle-aged woman he did not know.

Or not quite. He did know her as the most constant, faithful visitor in his hospital room; she'd made sure of that. The one who touched him when she didn't have to, kissed him when she left, the one for whom his recovery obviously mattered the most. From the first day, when he was unable to talk and could barely move, she was with him, tender and loyal.

The virus machines had been extracted, but the resultant functional memory loss, so far, was intractable and total. Fergus, aghast, had worked for weeks on the problem, but so far had nothing for them.

Vic knew they were married, because Clara had told him.

"Well." She put on a chipper face. "Shall we go home?"

"Yes. Home would be good."

Clara led Vic around their house, pointing out the drawers that stuck and the loose tile on the bathroom floor, feeling like she was showing it to a prospective buyer. Not wanting to overwhelm him all at once, she mentioned only a few of the things that had special meaning: the coral they'd brought back from Jamaica and the couch they'd spent two years arguing about before they bought it. Upstairs, on the way from the spare bedroom to the office they shared, he stopped suddenly in front of his fraternity composite photo.

"Look at that; I remember when we took this!" he said, a boyish glee on his face. "Wow, Tucker looks ridiculous! And Garrison, boy oh boy!" He laughed while he shook his head. "I wonder where they are now."

Clara considered a moment before answering. "Sid Garrison lives in New Haven. I'm afraid Bobby Tucker died of cancer, ten years ago."

Vic closed his eyes and inhaled sharply. She put her arms around him, but he shrugged her off after just long enough to let her know that he appreciated it.

In the bedroom, his gaze lingered for a moment on the flowery yellow comforter on the queen-size bed before looking away, embarrassed. Then he saw the photo on the wall.

"Wait — isn't that — " He walked up to it and squinted. "That looks just like the Orpheus Fountain, but it's not at Cranbrook!"

Clara swallowed. "Yes, it's in Stockholm. We saw it on our honeymoon."

"Whoa. And in the middle, that's supposed to be Orpheus?"

"Yes."

He shook his head slowly at the sculpture, his teeth on his lower lip. "Man, Milles was a genius, wasn't he? That's terrific." Then he said, "So, what else should I see?"

Vic was eager to help with the cooking, or even to take it over. That was familiar; Vic had always loved to cook. But of course he didn't know where anything was, and he did that stupid thing where he removed the green core from the garlic cloves, and he tried to use a serrated knife to slice meat. It made Clara a little nostalgic, recalling their first kitchen back in Hartford.

When he ripped the cork to shreds the first time he tried to use the corkscrew, she laughed and said, "I remember when you used to do that."

"Oh," he said, and changed the subject.

At eleven they went upstairs. Clara took off her blouse and put it in the hamper; she hung up her skirt. Standing in her underwear she glanced at Vic, who was opening the drawers at his dresser across the room and keeping his eyes away from her.

"Can't find the pajamas," he said.

She hesitated. "You, mm, usually sleep nude when we're together." He turned around and looked at her, surprise (and, she wasn't sure, maybe dismay) registering on his face. "So do I," she added. "Unless — would that make you uncomfortable?"

He shook his head quickly. "No, no, of course not. That's fine."

Suddenly she thought of how she would look to a 22-year-old man. Her belly sagged over the waistband of her panties; her hips and thighs were a rippling landscape. When her bra came off, her breasts would droop; little wrinkles and stretch marks were everywhere. Vic, her Vic, used to kiss and cherish each of these signs of her age separately, lingering with special tenderness at the curve of her belly, murmuring sentimental nonsense. But this boy in a man's body?

He didn't look at her as she finished undressing, and she tried not to stare as he got ready himself. When, as he pulled back the covers and climbed in beside her, she saw that he had the beginning of an erection, she wasn't sure whether she felt relief or something like a virgin's panic.

Clara propped herself on her elbow and put her hand on Vic's chest. He put his own hand on top of hers and let them both rest there for a few minutes, saying nothing — breathing and listening to each other breathe. Once or twice their eyes met, and he would make a smile that looked only a little forced; probably hers did too.

Then Clara licked her dry lips and said, "I don't want to rush you. I know this must be strange."

He swallowed, and she saw a look she knew well, a look he'd had even in the early days, the little wince when he realized she was unhappy. Then he looked her in the eyes. "It's been a long time for you, hasn't it? It must have been hard." Then he realized what he'd said, and an embarrassed puff of laughter escaped him. "I mean, you know, difficult."

"Yes."

He frowned, then took a breath like a man about to attempt the high dive. Then he smiled again, and this time it did not look forced. "I want to try."

The kiss was familiar and reassuring; Vic's lips and tongue explored hers the way they always had, and his hand on the back of her neck felt just as it should. Then he surprised her by putting his mouth to her nipple and beginning to nurse, something he hadn't done in years because he knew she didn't like it. She felt herself begin to resist and almost spoke, but decided not to; there would be time to teach him, to remind him of what worked and what didn't. This time, in bed with a woman whose body he knew not at all, let him explore her in the way he wanted.

It felt a little like she was having an affair, like this was a stranger instead of the husband she'd loved for half her life. It was awkward and made her a little shy, though she knew she needed to be the confident one tonight. But it was also unexpectedly exciting, and her body responded with a quickness that astonished her.

His hand fumbled between her legs, searching a strange land without a guide. He asked, "Is that okay?" and she gently pulled his fingers to a better place. "Try there," she said.

Sooner than she expected, she felt his weight shift, and he rolled on top of her. "Um, condom?" he asked, looking worried.

"IUD."

"Oh."

And suddenly he was in her, so suddenly that it would have hurt if she hadn't been so very ready. Of course he didn't know about her, and hadn't waited. She didn't remember anything so clumsy from their first nights together, but perhaps she had just replaced unpleasant memories with some she liked better.

He thrust with an urgency that seemed almost desperate, and she was barely able to begin moving in counterpoint before he climaxed and collapsed on her. She stroked the back of his neck.

When he stopped panting and was able to lift himself to look at her, he said, with a face so serious it was almost funny, "And how about you?"

Flustered, she said, "Um, no, I can't, I mean — " He looked crushed. "It's all right. Really. You didn't know. Next time I'll show you."

He nodded. "Okay." He chewed his lip as his hand fondled her breast. "I want to, you know? Not selfish, I mean, I've never *been* selfish that way — "

"No, no, you've never been selfish, not once. Or at least — " She found she was able to smirk. "At least you were selfish only when that made things more fun."

He nodded and squeezed her breast lightly. "Good. I'm glad." But he didn't look so very glad.

Before long he rolled off her and grabbed a tissue. He didn't get one for her, so she reached for the box on her own side of the bed. Vic snapped off his light, murmured "Good night," and was asleep within minutes.

When Clara started to cry, she told herself she was being ridiculous. What had she expected? He was still Vic, of course he was still Vic, but there was so much to rebuild. She had to be patient.

The thought did not comfort her, but she made sure that he wouldn't hear her.

♎

Laura Teng was ecstatic. "I remember painting *Trauma Tree!*" she crowed to Clara. "I remember looking at East Rock and thinking about how to frame it! I remember all of it!" She practically jumped up and down on the examining table. "I want to kiss you! Can I kiss you?"

Euphoria, Clara noted. *Side-effect?* Undeterred by her seizures or the accident at the first attempt to introduce the stimulators, Laura had readily agreed to a second round. With restraints in place, the administration had been flawless. Initially the impulse replication had seemed to have no effect, but after three weeks there had been a breakthrough.

Clara smiled. "Maybe later. Do you remember — " She paused. "Have you and Melissa explored the causes of the amnesia?"

A more solemn look came over Laura's face.. "Yes, and I think I remember that too. I'm — I'm not able — I'm talking about it with Melissa, you know? I don't think I can really —"

Clara touched Laura's arm. "Of course. That's the best way to handle it." *Emotional trauma*? she wrote. "We should do some really rigorous memory tests, see just how detailed your recollection is. Then we should do them again in a few days, to see whether the memories stick."

The results of the memory tests were astonishing, and there was no fall-off over three days, nor over six, twelve, or twenty-four. There were gaps, certainly, some of them significant, but the overall fabric of Laura's life was a single weave again. She was the person she remembered, the artist she remembered. The short-term euphoria faded, but the gratitude remained.

"Let me do something for you!" She said after the sixty-day follow-up visit. "For both of you, you and your husband. How about a painting? I'd love to make you a painting."

"It's not necessary," said Clara. "We've already been paid."

"It's not about *payment*. Let me give you a gift."

"Wouldn't you rather give a gift to Fergus Catherwood or Melissa?"

"I already am." Laura grinned. "Really. It would be such a pleasure."

"Well..." Clara considered. "Have you ever heard of the Orpheus Fountain?"

For their twenty-first anniversary, Clara presented Vic with Laura Teng's painting, which she had based both on photographs of the Stockholm installation and on Milles's original sketches. In Teng's vision, light pours from the face of Orpheus, touching each of the eight listeners; the ray to Beethoven is especially bright. The image carries with it the inspiration of one generation to the next, repeating throughout history. But there is no trace of Orpheus's grief; so far as this painting is concerned, Eurydice might never have existed.

Vic smiled and kissed her and told her it was beautiful. At that same dinner, he gave Clara a copy of Sherwin Nuland's *Doctors: The Biography of Medicine*. She had read it three or four times already; they first read it together in medical school. It was the sort of gift people gave to doctors. She smiled and kissed him and told him it was thoughtful.

Afterwards they made love. Vic had paid attention to Clara's hints and suggestions and was now proficient at doing what her body wanted. But he approached the task with workmanlike concentration, not with passionate devotion. For her part, Clara had recalled things that used to please Vic in the old days, and they still did. But when she tried something he'd liked at thirty-five or forty, he was grateful for the effort, but no more.

Neither of them mentioned the anniversary presents again, except that, a week later, Clara asked Vic whether she could put the painting of the Orpheus Fountain next to the photograph. He said, "Sure."

She had begun to get used to the fact that they now needed to take turns in conversation. For one thing, they wanted to discuss different topics: she lacked his renewed enthusiasm for competitive sailing, which he'd given up five years after they were married. He had none of her interest in fine arts, and had little to say when she went on about gallery shows. But more than this, the *rhythm* of their conversation was different; Vic was more inclined to interrupt, to rush to the next point, to change the subject at random. Clara wanted to meander, to explore the nooks and crannies of a topic, to circle back to the beginning and see how it looked. She didn't remember this difference between them in the old days; in fact, their conversations had always been one of the sensual delights of their marriage.

So they listened politely to each other, making sympathetic sounds and trying, really trying, to find meaningful things to say in response. Each of them felt that they were walking on the deck of a ship made of paper, and that one misstep would plunge them both into the sea.

♎

Eight months after their anniversary, Clara came home from the hospital to find Vic studying medical school catalogues. Of course his degree was meaningless now; he wanted to fulfill his original intention and go through training again, even if it meant graduating when he was 50 and completing his residency at 54.

Clara sat down across from Vic, setting her coat on the back of the chair; the hem dragged on the floor. She said, "Fergus thinks he's cracked the code on what happened to you in the accident. He says he can design a new series of implants that will allow you to access the memories that are blocked."

Vic said, still looking at the catalogues, "Not sure I should trust Catherwood to fix what he broke in the first place."

She made a sympathetic sound in her throat. "I understand how you feel. But what's the alternative? No one's advanced as far as he has with this treatment, and he's studied your case inside and out."

Vic still didn't look up. "I was thinking that we could just leave well enough alone."

There was a pause. Clara repeated, "Well enough alone."

"Sure. I'm all right the way I am. Body's older, but it would be anyway."

"But — but *twenty years*, Vic. All that you learned, all those people; your life was so rich . . ."

He did not say anything. He flipped through the catalogue, but both of them knew he wasn't reading it.

"It would be a time saver," she said in a lighter tone. "You could save all those years of neurology residency."

"Actually," he said. "I'm not sure I want to go into neurology. You never know, but there are some really interesting things going on in oncology now, I've heard."

She swallowed. "Yes." Then she reached over and put her hand on his arm. For the first time, he looked her in the eyes.

"My husband," she said, not addressing him but conjuring. "Vic. My husband. Please."

There was another pause. They heard the wind against the windows of the house.

"I think — " Vic's voice wasn't steady, and he tried again. "I think he's gone, Clara. I don't think he's coming back. I mean, I don't think I want him back."

Clara did not say anything. She looked around the kitchen, at all the familiar things she could have found with her eyes shut. She did not look at him.

Ω

She woke up earlier than usual. Through the crack in the blinds, Clara could see a strip of eastern sky, blending from sapphire to an orange horizon, the last moment of a perfect painting. As she watched, the first flash of sunrise destroyed the fragile balance of the twilight; she turned away and blinked, clearing her vision.

She wrapped herself in her robe, shivering a little in the brief time it took the cool fabric to steal some of the warmth from her skin. In the hallway she saw that the door to the extra bedroom was still shut; she padded downstairs carefully, so as not to disturb Vic, if he was still sleeping. But when she carried her coffee to the office across from her bedroom, she heard his footsteps in the attic.

They continued while she checked her e-mail and began working on the household accounts.

She heard him descend the drop-down staircase. Then he was at the door to the office, an apologetic look on his face.

"Can you show me which suitcases are mine?" he asked.

It didn't take Vic long to pack; he wanted only his clothes and his fraternity composite photo. The other possessions in the house, the ones they'd accumulated together, were going to stay with her. As he was snapping the latch on the last suitcase, Clara came into the bedroom and asked him, "Do you want the Orpheus Fountain?"

He frowned up at the photo and the painting — looking, for a moment, like Orpheus himself.

"No. You keep them."

He embraced her before he left, their arms bumping awkwardly as sometimes happens when strangers try to hug each other before they are really ready.

For three months both versions of the Orpheus Fountain looked down at Clara from the foot of her bed. Then, one Friday evening before she undressed, she wrapped them in old newspapers and set them gently in the attic.

At Clarion, Robert Crais asked us to write an explicit sex scene between two characters who knew each other well. I misunderstood and wrote a scene in which the sex itself showed *how well the characters knew each other. Immediately I wanted to write another scene in which the sex showed that the same characters* didn't *know each other, and shortly afterwards decided to tell how they forgot.*

Like Vic, I attended the Cranbrook School and saw the duplicate Orpheus Fountain nearly every day for six years. The summer after college, I backpacked around northern Europe and found myself in Stockholm, where I came upon the original fountain with no preparation. I stood with my mouth open for twenty minutes; I can't remember whether I wept.

— KLS

Keeping Tabs

I was so excited when I could finally buy a Tab. They cost so much, you know, but I saved up for maybe six months. I waitressed at Antonio's in the North End, and let me tell you, it's murder on the feet. Those trays are heavy, too, and Nico screams at everybody the whole shift, not to mention the way you smell after six hours. But the customers tip really well, and I was able to save up enough money, even after paying rent and stuff.

I could never have gotten a Tab when I was still married to Marc, that shit. He never liked anything I liked. When I married him, all I saw was the big brown eyes and the cleft in his chin and the way he could make his voice go down low, so that I felt it all the way down to my knees. I had to learn the hard way.

Not that I could've afforded a Tab back then, anyway. The price started coming down just a few years ago, about when Marc broke my front tooth. By that time I couldn't go to my mom's, because she said I always went back to that shit anyway, and she wasn't going to help me do it again, and my friend Lila wouldn't let me stay with her either, same reason. So I went to a shelter, and the police came, and we got a restraining order on Marc. But yeah, the same damn thing happened, he gave me that look with those eyes and told me how things were really, really going to change this time, because he'd seen the light and couldn't believe he'd done something like that to me, and like an asshole, I dropped the charges and lifted the restraining order and went back to him.

Two years ago, right after I divorced Marc, Pearl Moulton started playing Mandi Trenton on *Dark Little Corners*, which was her first really big break, and they announced that there'd be a Tab on her. I wanted it as soon as I saw her on the show, because Mandi is so awesome; she's this really tough girl who works in a bar, and she gives as good as she gets, and she never gives up on love when all these guys leave her all the time. And Pearl Moulton is so beautiful and talented; I used to watch her on *Deception*, when nobody paid her any attention. Now she was in all the magazines, and she's exactly my age, and she was Tabbed.

But then my mom got sick, and I was taking care of her for two months. My brother Johnny didn't do squat, and his wife Nadine, forget it. So I wasn't able to get the Tab until she got better. That was last year, in May.

I got the injection and the ear cuff, went home and waited for Pearl Moulton's Tab time, which was ten to twelve, Eastern. I was so excited I couldn't sit down; I kept making cups of coffee and forgetting to drink them, picking up the *Herald* and reading stuff I'd already read. Finally it was ten, and I sat down in the recliner and turned on the cuff.

First thing, while it was making the connection, it was like I didn't have a body at all — no sight, no sound, no feeling, nothing. It's a good thing your body breathes by itself, because I couldn't even tell if I was. Then, all of a sudden, wham, I was in this padded chair, and I had Pearl Moulton's body. She's a lot thinner than I am, and her teeth are really straight, and you feel those things right away. At first there was no sound and I couldn't see anything, but there was this sweet smell, and something soft brushing down over my face, that is, her face.

Then a girl's voice said, "Okay, done," and Pearl opened her eyes and blew out through her nose, like there was dust in it. She was sitting in a swivel chair in front of a big mirror like they have at a salon, with vanity bulbs all around it. In the mirror Pearl looked exactly like Mandi Trenton on *Dark Little Corners*, right down to the funny arch in the eyebrow. I'll tell you, looking in the mirror and seeing Mandi was the best feeling in the world, although it only lasted for a second.

Standing behind Pearl was a girl with striped hair and a gold nose ring; she put down a soft brush she was holding and undid the sheet that was covering Pearl's clothes. Underneath Pearl was wearing one of those green outfits Mandi Trenton has in the program.

Pearl said, "Thanks, Victoria," and it was like I was saying it. Then she stood up, and it was like I was standing up, and she walked out the door.

It's really weird to feel somebody else's mouth saying words, and to hear the sound of her voice in her head. You know how your own voice, when you talk, never sounds the way it does when somebody records it and plays it back? Well, Pearl Moulton's voice doesn't sound the same in her head either. It's also pretty strange to feel somebody else's feet when she walks, or hands when she grabs things. I mean, *my* body was sitting in the recliner in my living room, and if I tried to lift Pearl's hand I'd wind up lifting my own off the arm of the chair, but I wouldn't feel it. And of course she doesn't walk the way I do; she takes quicker steps, and each step is exactly in front of the other one, like she was walking the line for a cop. She's taller than I am too, and everything looks different from that angle.

Pearl clickety-clicked into a huge Vid stage with big hot lights and two of the sets from *Dark Little Corners*, the nightclub and Mandi's bedroom. A bunch of people said, "Morning, Pearl," and she said "Hi, guys." It was weird, and great, to hear her say something so normal. She grabbed a bottle of water off a table and sat down in one of those folding chairs, just like you see in the movies.

And then not much happened for a while. First she was looking at the script, then she read a magazine she picked up off the floor next to the chair. It's totally impossible to read with somebody else's eyes, let me tell you. I mean, Pearl moved her eyes to follow what she wanted to see right then, which was nothing like the way I would have moved my eyes when I was reading. Not that I would have read this magazine anyway; it was a complicated story about all those poor people getting killed in Turkey, and whether that counts as genocide, and what genocide is, and stuff like that. But like I say, I couldn't even see most of the words; it was mostly a jerky jumble. And did you know, Pearl Moulton has itchy skin, especially near the armpits? I would have been scratching like crazy, but it didn't seem to bother her. Or, I don't know, maybe it did bother her and she just didn't scratch.

So then some guy said, "Pearl, Randy, we're ready for you." And Pearl walked onto the nightclub set, and so did Randall James! He's really short, shorter than Pearl, anyway, although he doesn't look like it on the show. But he's got pretty brown eyes and a dimple. They did a scene where Mandi and Mace are arguing about some woman Mace went out with the night before, and Mandi smacks him and cries, and Mace walks out in a huff. Pearl really hit him, too, but not hard.

They did this scene nine or ten times, and in between they'd wait while the guys messed with the lights and moved the cameras around or played with light meters, and the two of them talked about a party that they were going to go to at Zero-Zero-Zero that night. Pearl said that Tim — you know she's married to Timothy Nation, who played the guy on *Deception*? — she said that Tim didn't really want to go, and didn't want her to go without him, but that she was going to make him come. Can you imagine a party at Zero-Zero-Zero?

I used to think they shot soaps live, and I guess they did in the old days. But later I found out that they have better editing and stuff than they used to, and they can do lots of takes and put them together in a hurry. But it was so much fun just being there, with all the actors and everybody.

Somewhere in the middle of ninth or tenth take on that scene, the Tab ended and I was back in my recliner. It took me a few minutes to get used to me again. Nothing like living in the body of a thin, beautiful actress to make you feel fat and ugly when you get home. I saw myself in the mirror; I looked about as good as I usually do, which is not very.

I had to go to work. On the way to the T stop, I tried putting one foot right in front of the other, like I was walking on a line.

Nico was especially nasty to all the waitresses that day, and Lila cried after a customer screamed at her about an order that wasn't her fault. Rob, the snotty kid who runs the Hobart in the afternoons, broke a teacup, and I thought Nico was going to have a heart attack. "Do you know how much costs a cup?" he kept yelling. Rob didn't flinch the whole time, looking down his long nose at Nico.

It was kind of hot for May, too, and Nico hadn't had the air conditioning fixed, so we were all sweating. I left with my uniform sticking all over me, making me itch; I scratched on the T all the way home.

Some people get Tabs at the same time every week, but they cost a lot more. Mine was the cheapest, and they scheduled me whenever they could fit me in, and I only found out a few days before; sometimes it was too late for me to arrange the time, and I missed it. For instance, my second Tab time for Pearl Moulton was five days after the first one, at four o'clock Eastern, so I couldn't Tab her because I was at work. The time after that, I had to go fight with the landlord, because a pipe burst in the apartment over mine and I had disgusting, dirty water in my cabinets and dishes, and half the food in the pantry was ruined. It was the third time something like that happened.

When I finally I got a chance to Tab Pearl again, it was in the middle of the day on a Saturday — middle of the day for her, afternoon for me. She was at home with Timothy Nation, and she was cooking in her kitchen. I think I would have liked it better if she was on the set doing Mandi Trenton again, but this was good too. Her kitchen is huge, with a stone island in the middle and spotlights shining down on it. She was cooking something with a lot of vegetables in it: zucchini, eggplant, onions, peppers, tomatoes, garlic, all in big chunks and thrown in to this gigantic pot. It reminded me of the Italian cooking my mom used to do, but I don't think Pearl is Italian.

Halfway through the chopping, Tim came up behind her and kissed the back of her neck, and she said "Hi," in that kind of low voice you use on someone you like. Then he brought his arms around her middle and kissed her ear, which tickled, and she put down the knife and leaned back into him, kind of laughing, you know, chuckling.

Then his hands came up to her tits, and she gasped and stuck her elbow in his stomach, and said, "No, Tim! The Tab!"

He said, "Shit, I forgot," and backed away from her — she almost lost her balance. Then he said, "Can't they at least make it the same days and times every week, so that we could remember? You're not a slave."

She said, "I tried again on Monday. They won't budge. I'm sorry."

Then he walked out of the room. I could tell Pearl was mad after that, because she started chopping down harder on the vegetables. The stew or whatever it was she was making took a long time to cook (it smelled awesome), but she stayed in the kitchen the whole time, reading another one of those magazines I couldn't read. Tim Nation didn't come back in the kitchen. I wonder how the stew tasted.

Now, so you don't get the wrong idea, I don't get off on the sex thing with the Tab. I know there are some perverts — guys — who would get Tabs on somebody like Pearl Moulton so that they could feel her body. But the hookers downtown would let you Tab them for a lot less money, and if you were that kind of pervert and you paid them enough, they would do all kinds of stuff to themselves while you were Tabbed into them. But the real sickos want to know what it feels like to have Pearl Moulton's tits in particular, you know? I heard that some of the actresses got sex-limited Tabs, that they'd only let other women Tab them. But I don't know if Pearl was one of them.

I got to Tab Pearl three or four times during the next six months or so. I had a lot of time on the set of *Dark Little Corners*, which was my favorite;

it was like being an actress and being Mandi Trenton all at the same time. Other times, like parties or times at home or when she was having lunch with a friend, I got the idea that Pearl didn't like the Tab so well. She would tell people not to talk about certain things because of the Tab, and she had this angry sound in her voice. Tim Nation didn't like it either, and he got madder and madder every time she would say stuff like that. Once he threw a glass into the sink so hard it broke. But me, I thought the Tab was terrific. I was having the time of my life.

In December I heard that they were going to start a TalkBack feature, where one Tabber at a time would be actually able to say things to the person they were Tabbing. It's a lot more expensive than the Tab itself; it would take me months to save enough tips for even one two-hour TalkBack. But boy, did I want it. To be able to talk to Pearl Moulton!

At about the same time my Mom got sick again, and then my brother Johnny got sick too, and Nadine just walked out on him, if you can believe it. After all the help he didn't give me with Mom the first time, I didn't really feel like lifting a finger for Johnny, but what could I do? He's a lazy bum and he always has been, but he was going to chemo and he needed me. Between the diarrhea and the puking and me taking care of Mom too, let me tell you, January and February sucked.

I got only a few chances to go on the Tab during all that time, and they were all stuff like eating meals and press conferences. She likes to eat stuff I never tried, like sushi and spicy Vietnamese cabbage and tofu. I wonder if it tasted the same to her as it tasted to me. I didn't like it much, so I guess not.

♎

In April I was Tabbing Pearl when she was having drinks with Tim Nation and one of the directors she works with, Donny Blanchette. All of a sudden she said, "Stop it. Shut up." Blanchette looked at her and asked what he said wrong. Pearl said, "Not you, the Tab. They've got the TalkBack on me now, and I have a woman in Sydney talking to me." Then she stopped for a second like she was listening, and said, "No, I *know* you paid for it. But I'm trying to have drinks with my friends, and I can't concentrate with you talking in my head." She stopped again. "I'll talk to you later, I promise. Just, please, stop talking to me now. Please?"

"Should have gone out later," said Tim Nation, like it was her fault.

"When?" said Pearl, and I felt her throat get tight the way it does when you're trying not to cry. "If I'm not filming or sleeping, I'm on the Tab."

"That's an exaggeration," said Tim, but he looked mad.

"It's like I have no life of my own," said Pearl, and by this time her eyes were getting blurry, and they stung.

"No," said Blanchette. "It's that *they* have no lives of their own."

Donny Blanchette is a prick. Okay, that girl shouldn't have been talking while Pearl was having drinks with Tim. I said to myself that I would never do that when I got the TalkBack. But who does Blanchette think he is, with his "They have no lives of their own"? Let Donny Blanchette take a look at my Mom, or at my brother, or at my job with Nico, or at this stinking apartment. This is what life *is*; what the hell does he think *he's* got? Does he think that's *real*?

♎

I was finally able to afford the TalkBack this May, but the waiting list was three months long before I could actually have my TalkBack session with Pearl. But I got the feature installed right away, because I knew that you had to get taught how to use it. Talking with your mouth doesn't work, because for one thing, you can't feel your mouth when you're Tabbing, and the person you're Tabbing can't hear your voice anyway. You have to picture saying the words in your head, and there's this feature that lets you hear the words you're saying, and the tone of voice and everything. But it takes practice. You can turn it on without Tabbing, so I worked on it the whole time, practicing saying things. Mostly I was saying *You're awesome, Pearl*, or stuff like that, but I did work on longer sentences too.

Meanwhile I came down with pneumonia and missed a lot of work, and then Nico fired me. Lila said that I could sue him, but I didn't have the time for stuff like that; I just needed to get another job. So finally I went to work at Tomas's, which is in a different part of town. The tips weren't as good, but I could get along. If I hadn't already paid for the TalkBack, I wouldn't have been able to afford it anymore.

Not too long after I got the TalkBack set up, weird stuff started happening with the Tab.

One time I was Tabbing Pearl while she was shopping at L'Oiseau Blanc, which is this tiny shop she likes, and all of a sudden I couldn't hear anything — I mean I couldn't hear anything that was happening around *Pearl*; I could hear the jackhammer outside my own window just fine. That lasted for maybe fifteen minutes, then stopped. Another time she was on a talk show, and in the middle of a question I stopped feeling her body. I could still see the lights and hear the questions and smell the make-up, but all I could feel was my own butt on the recliner.

I called Customer Service, and they said that they hadn't had any other reports like that, and that it sounded like a fluke, and was I *sure* the sound and touch had gone out? And they said they'd call me back, and they never did. Pricks.

In June I found out that Marc got married again. Honest to God, I wanted to find out the girl's name, call her up and warn her. She was going to be a punching bag, and she didn't know. I told Lila, and she rolled her eyes and said, "You think the new wife is going to believe the ex about anything?"

"I could show her the police report and the restraining order."

"She'll never talk to you, and if she does then Marc will have some smooth story about how you gave as good as you got, and it was all a set-up. She's not going to listen to you."

And then, right that second, I couldn't hear Lila anymore. I heard Pearl's voice, like I was in her head, yelling, "Goddam it, Randy, that's the twelfth time we've done it! Jesus Christ!"

Then I heard Randall James say, "Sorry, Pearl; I don't know what's wrong with me today." Then Donny Blanchette's voice started talking, and I heard them starting to do a scene.

At first Lila was still trying to talk to me, but then she saw my face (I guess I looked pretty spooked) and came around the table and held my hands and said stuff I couldn't hear. She looked scared out of her socks. It took ten minutes before I could hear her again.

It happened again later that day, but with my vision. For about five minutes all I could see was Tim Nation in their bedroom. He looked like he was yelling, and was red in the face and moving his hands a lot. But I couldn't hear anything.

This time Customer Service actually listened to me. They told me to come right to the service center on Tremont Street. The technician looked almost as worried as I was. Neither of those two times had even been one of Pearl's scheduled Tab sessions, and I wasn't wearing the ear cuff, it was in my bag. So the techie did some deal where he replaced the "neural links" or something, and he said that should take care of it.

Johnny's chemo wasn't working, and in July we found out that the cancer had spread to his liver. Nadine came back and started taking care of him, and she wasn't hysterical or anything. When I went over to their house and she and I were alone, she'd cry a little on my shoulder, but that was all. Johnny was handling it pretty good too, kidding me and joking about surgery. I don't think I could have made jokes, if it was me. They said there might be a chance of a liver transplant, but there was a long waiting list.

But the techie was wrong about the problem being fixed. It happened again right after Nadine moved back in with Johnny. I woke up at about one in the morning, and I couldn't feel my body. I could see my room, and hear the traffic, but what I felt was Pearl walking back and forth really fast, pounding her hands on hard things so that they hurt. Her throat was sore, like she'd been yelling, and her face felt hot. Then I felt somebody's hand grab her arm —

Her nose, my nose, crunched and hurt so bad I couldn't see. Then there was a slap on my mouth, and something warm on her tongue —

It was like I was back with Marc, and he was smashing me in the face and screaming. I could remember every moment, every fight, every punch. But it wasn't happening to me; I was in my bed alone. It was Pearl. It was all happening to Pearl.

I felt a shove in her chest, and she fell over, and something hard hit the side of her head, and then I think I felt a kick in her stomach —

Then it cut off, and I was just me.

I got up and ran for the phone, but before I could get there I threw up in the kitchen.

A girl dispatcher answered: "9-1-1. What is the emergency you are reporting?"

"Tim Nation is beating up Pearl Moulton!"

"Where is this emergency taking place?"

"In California, I think. It's wherever they have their house."

She stopped for a second. Then she said, "You think? Where are you located?"

"I'm in Boston."

"Massachusetts?"

"Yes."

She stopped again. Then, "Did you witness this event yourself?"

"Yes, I'm Tabbing Pearl Moulton."

"This happened while she was on the Tab?"

"No, not exactly, it's not her Tab time."

"But you witnessed her being beaten?"

"Yes. The Tab is broken! I'm Tabbing her when I'm not supposed to."

There was a muffled sound, like she was covering the phone and talking to someone.

Then she said, "Is the event still occurring now?"

"I don't know; I think so."

"Is anyone hurt, or in need of medical attention?"

"Yes! Pearl Moulton is hurt!"

"What is your name, address and phone number?"

I gave them to her, and she said she would follow up on it, then she hung up.

I tried to sleep, but I couldn't. The next day I called Customer Service again, and this time the techie I saw was a girl, and she said she could take out the whole Tab just to be sure. I told her no, just change it like last time. I know it sounds stupid, but the TalkBack time was coming up in just a few weeks, and now I needed to talk to Pearl more than ever.

No one from 9-1-1 or the police or anybody ever called me back. There was nothing in the magazines or the Vids about Pearl the next week, except that she cancelled a talk show appearance and there was something about her missing a few days of shooting on the set because of "illness." There was no news about Timothy Nation either.

Finally came the day in August. I sat down on the recliner, put on the cuff, and took a deep breath; my heart was going pretty fast. Then I switched it on.

Pearl was washing her face in her bathroom. The water was too hot, and I wanted to wince when it splashed over her closed eyes and into her nostrils. She blew the water out of her nose and smooshed her face into a thick towel. Then she opened her eyes and looked in the mirror.

There were no bruises on her that I could see, and I didn't feel any pain at all. If her nose was broken, it didn't feel like it and didn't look like it. Could they fix all that in a month? Her mouth was tight, and I could feel the muscles in her cheeks. Then she turned her head, and I caught a faint spot of yellow on the side of her face, where I remembered she hit the floor.

Hello, Pearl, I said.

"I don't really feel like talking right now," she said. "Sorry." She walked into the bedroom, barefoot, and started putting on her shoes.

You need to leave Tim, I said.

She stopped, and I could feel her eyes get wide. "That's a hell of a thing to say."

I'm the one who called 9-1-1.

She closed her eyes; I couldn't see. "I don't know what you're talking about."

Yes, yes you do! I know all about this stuff! It happened to me too, I can tell you how to —

"You can't tell me anything! You don't know me; you don't know us! You have nothing; you have no lives of your own, any of you, so you suck it all out of me. Leave me alone, can't you?"

No, please, Pearl! This is really important. You're in danger, and I can help you!

Her eyes opened again and she got up and went to the window. It was so bright outside that her eyes hurt, but she didn't close them.

"Listen to me. Listen! I need you not to interfere in my life. In *any* part of my life, do you understand? All you people, you say you care about me, but you don't. If you really did, you'd let me be."

I do care about you, I care so much! I can't let it happen to you, not what happened to me!

"Listen, whoever you are —"

Dorothy. Telling her my name made me want to cry.

"Whoever. I'm sorry about what happened to you, but it has nothing to do with me."

It does. You know it does.

"Please, for God's sake, listen to me. Do you know what's worse, even worse than that?"

Nothing, I was sure. But I said, *What?*

"Having no privacy, no moment to yourself. Being eaten alive by people who say they love you. That's the worst thing in the world — being hurt in the name of love."

I couldn't feel my eyes or nose, but by now I knew I must be crying. *I do love you, Pearl. I love you! Let me save you.*

"No one can save anyone," she whispered. "But if you love me, you know how you can prove it. There's only one thing I want."

So there it was, that's who I was. There were two of us, Tim Nation and me. Tim she could run away from, but I was in her head, like a bad memory.

I stopped talking. I didn't say anything for the rest of the TalkBack session. I'll never be able to afford another one.

♎

I stopped Tabbing Pearl Moulton. I had to take the Tab out anyway; I couldn't be sure it wouldn't break again, and I didn't want sudden looks at her life anymore.

Pearl is still living with Tim Nation; that's what the *Herald* says. I don't know if she ever saw a counselor, or what.

Johnny's going to die. The doctors say the cancer is "inoperable." I've been spending a lot of time at their house; Nadine is a wreck, but she manages. She holds my hand a lot while we're over there. Mom's not doing too well either, but I think Johnny's cancer is harder on her than what she's got herself. She comes over to their house too, but she just cries, which drives Nadine crazy, so sometimes Nadine comes over here when Mom's with Johnny.

We've talked about a hospice, but he wants to die at home, in private. So would I, I think, if it was me.

When I try to ignore the tabloids in the grocery line, I'm fascinated by our apparently unlimited thirst to learn about the private lives of strangers. I began to wonder how far people would take it if they could.

I was angry while writing the first draft, and originally intended Dorothy to be the clueless antagonist. But she grew on me (possibly because I based her speech patterns on someone I was fond of 25 years ago), until I realized that she was the hero.

An example of how much a first reader can influence the work: I workshopped this story at Clarion, and one of my classmates said that it reminded her of Philip K. Dick, "except that, in Dick, the technology would break.*" The last half of the revised story grew out of that remark.*

— KLS

Hear the Enemy, My Daughter

Everything about Kesi reminds me of her father. Her hair is crinklier than mine, because Jabari's was. Her skin is a darker shade of brown than mine, because Jabari's was. Her chin juts out absurdly for such a little face, because Jabari's did. She even smells like him. Every sight of her is like a kick in my stomach.

Kesi has stopped wondering where Jabari has gone. For the first two or three months, she asked many times a day, "Mzazi, where Baba?" She was past such baby-talk; it was a sign of her distress that she regressed, lost her verbs. I was honest with her, or I tried to be. You can say, "Baba has died. Baba was very brave, he was fighting to protect Kesi and Mzazi, he was fighting to protect everyone." But how much of that will a three-year-old understand? All she knew was that her father was gone. I did not even tell her that he had gone to a better place, that he was happy — what would be the point, even if I believed it? Did she care whether he was happy, if it kept him away forever?

Nor did I allow the other voice to speak, the voice that said, "I should have been fighting next to Jabari; I could have saved Jabari. If you had not been born, Jabari would still be here."

Now she is four and does not mention him at all. She remembers him; when I point to his picture, she tells me who Jabari is. But she does not begin conversation about him. She does not ask when he will return. She does not ask what it means to die.

♎

No matter how many times I watched them, the battle recordings told me nothing. The one identifiable word was the one we already knew: *kri'ikshi*, the one the Sheshash say over and over in combat. No commands, no calls to each other, just that same sound, *kri'ikshi*. Nothing in the recordings explained its meaning, nor gave any clue to the syntax of the rest of the Sheshash language, if language it was. With a frustrated sigh, I turned back to the latest pattern analysis on the intercepted signals between their ships, which so far had proved equally fruitless.

The call from Levi came just as I was getting ready to abandon the intractable recordings and go home to Kesi.

"We need you in Interrogation tomorrow, Halima," he said. "Can you handle it?"

I stiffened. "Of course, sir. I do my duty."

He made an impatient sound. "You know what I mean. I can get someone else, do some sort of swap, if I have to. Are you ready for this?"

He was right to ask, but it still annoyed me. After my combat tour, I used to feel an urge to get out of my chair whenever I saw a picture of a Sheshash. Those feelings subsided after Kesi was born, only to return with horror and rage after we lost Jabari on Heraclea. For a while, it was all I could do not to put my hand through the screen; once I actually did so, cutting my palm as I screamed.

But a year had gone by since Heraclea, and I was better, mostly better. I took a deep breath and visualized looking into the eyes of a Sheshash across a transparent barrier, talking to it, *smelling* it. My gorge did not rise, my heartbeat did not race.

"Yes, I'm ready. But I didn't know we had any Sheshash in Holding. Was there a new capture?"

"Oh yes, on Asculum, a spectacular one. We've actually got our hands on a fighting pair."

♎

No Sheshash fights alone. Always there are pairs of them, a three-meter giant and a half-meter dwarf, tens of thousands of pairs on the field at once. The larger and the smaller soldier fight with a rapid coordination that makes the mind swim and the eyes ache. When one moves, the other moves at the same millisecond; the recordings show literally that brief a delay, if delay it is. Any human soldier will be faced with the choice of fighting the giant or the dwarf, typically on opposite sides of him, and whichever he does not fight, that one will kill him.

Of course they cannot outrun projectiles or beam weapons any more than we can, but they do outrun the reflexes of human soldiers; they move faster than we can think. Artillery and bombs are effective, but after the first engagement the Sheshash never amassed enough troops in one location for ordnance to do much damage.

The dwarf member of a fighting pair is deadlier, more reckless than the giant. Both Sheshash use their weapons swiftly, cleanly, not wasting a calorie of energy. Nor do they seem to fight for advantage or position, to gain the high ground or keep the initiative. They kill as many as they can, do not stop trying to slaughter us until they are killed themselves or forcibly restrained.

No fighting pair had ever been captured before. We had taken giant Sheshash on the battlefield, either wounded or surrounded, but never had one of the dwarf fighters been taken prisoner, and surely no pair. On the battlefield we found approximately as many of the giant Sheshash slain as the dwarfs, but we never saw a smaller one alive unless it was still trying to kill us.

Many theories were proposed for this discrepancy. Some suggested that the dwarfs, being less strong, were expendable — but this made no sense in light of how much more effective killers they were. Others speculated that there was a class distinction between giant and dwarf, as between an officer and an enlisted soldier, or between a lord and a commoner. A simpler explanation was that the dwarf Sheshash were simply easier to kill. But detailed tabulations of battle recordings failed to show such a discrepancy in our hits. Indeed, there was a discrepancy the other way, as the larger fighters were easier targets. Instead, these recordings showed smaller Sheshash collapsing in the middle of a fight, with no apparent wound or impact. More, they showed that the dwarfs who collapsed were all fighting alone. When a pair was fighting together, neither of them underwent this spontaneous implosion.

All of our efforts at communication had so far been futile, and the Sheshash continued to attack at every opportunity. The High Command had considered evacuating all of our colonized worlds — probably not feasible before the Sheshash exterminated us on half-a-dozen of them. And in any case, since we didn't know why they were fighting us in the first place, for all we knew they would go on to finish the job on Terra.

We weren't without options. We had fusion bombs and atmospheric catalysts. We could stop them. The question was how to do it without committing genocide.

When I entered the cell, there was only one Sheshash present, a giant. As many as I have seen on the battlefield, they still astonish me. Their smooth, shiny skin is so bright a white it hurts the eyes, with a faint chartreuse overlay that appears and disappears like the rainbows of oil droplets in a puddle. Their three legs, slender and lithe, each have three major joints, rotating on dual axes like their three arms. Their three eyes are large and dark, like those of a seal. In combat those eyes open wide; at rest, as in captivity, they are typically half-closed, so the Sheshash give the impression of being perpetually sleepy. In a Sheshash who has lost its fighting partner, the eyes dart back and forth, up and down in a way that seems frantic to us. Perhaps this is the way they register grief or distress; perhaps the wide eyes signify anger.

Or perhaps we anthropomorphize even to ascribe these emotions to them. Our anger comes from the part of our brain that is reptilian, our grief from something somewhat later. But with an alien, how can you make such a comparison? Do they even have "reptilian brains?"

In the moment before it saw me, I had the feeling (justified or not) that the Sheshash was calm, even happy in the cell. It was moving slowly, its eyes in their half-shut position, and uttering a sound which, although high to our ears, was low for them.

Then the Sheshash noticed me. It moved rapidly forward with its arms out as if to attack, its eyes opening wide, but stopped before it hit the barrier. I backed away, beginning to reach for my weapon until I caught myself; I felt a sudden flush.

The Shesash pushed and tapped the barrier several times, using different combinations of its limbs until satisfied that there was no way it could get at me, or I at it. I stared at it for several seconds, and it gazed with half-closed eyes at me.

I swallowed, then phoned Levi.

"You told me there were two Sheshash in the cell. A fighting pair, yo said," I began.

"Wait a minute. We've been monitoring the cell. Just wait a minut you'll see. This is huge."

As I watched, a head poked out from the horizontal slit in the Sheshash belly. It was another Sheshash, the small one.

I did not gasp aloud. Holding the phone close to my mouth, I whispere "They are *marsupials*?"

"Who knows?" said Levi. "*If* the small one is a child, if the large one its mother—"

"Or father?"

"Parent, whatever. *If* the sack has a developmental function like tl marsupial pouch, then sure, why not, you can call them marsupials."

"Which still would not explain their reproduction," I said, as if mattered.

"Right," said Levi. "But it would tell us that they put their childre into combat."

Then the dwarf Sheshash's eyes opened fully and it shot out of tl pouch, throwing itself at the barrier to get at me. I didn't back away th time, but felt my heart pound in my chest. The dwarf bounced off tl barrier but tried again, bounced again and kept trying. Its mouth was ope and it was uttering the shriek we had heard on every battlefield: *Kri'iksh Kri'ikshi!*

The giant reached for the dwarf, but the dwarf seemed fully intent o me and would not be distracted, as if it did not understand that it coul not reach me.

Finally the giant uttered some long words; their voices are high an their language has a staccato quality to it. The dwarf Sheshash stoppe what it was doing, half-closed its eyes, and turned to the giant.

"*Kri'ikshi!*" it said. Its voice was even higher; it sounded like a whistl

"*Kri'ikshi sha'akdash kishidi to'ishati*," said the giant.

"*Kri'ikshi! Kri'ikshi!*" the dwarf repeated, spinning a circle around tl big one.

"*Kri'ikshi sha'akdash*," the giant said again, more slowly, each soun pronounced more precisely. "*Kri'ikshi Kishidi. Kri'ikshi to'ishati.*"

"*Kri'ikshi*," the little one repeated, more quietly. But it stopped movin

"*Shi*," said the big one. Then the dwarf hopped up and crawled back into the pouch. It squirmed its way down (like someone burrowing into warm blankets, I thought) and became quiescent. Its eyes closed.

It seemed obvious. The little Sheshash was more excitable, more likely to attack, less likely to understand the concept of a transparent barrier, than the big one. Its vocabulary was more limited, or else it had a less nuanced use of it. It understood that I was the enemy and wanted to kill me. The giant had tried to make it understand — what? That they were prisoners? That there was a barrier? That killing me would accomplish nothing? — and had had a hard time getting the message across. But the smaller one — the *child* — became docile anyway, and returned to the larger one's — its *mother's* — pouch. Once there, it fell asleep.

We had no clue as to their gender, and the exact relationship might not even be familial. But my instinct said: mother and child.

♎

Kesi's use of language misleads me into thinking she has a mind like mine. She uses a subject, verb, and object in ways I understand, and so I imagine that she means by it the same thing I would mean. But a four-year-old, in some ways, is as different from an adult as a chimpanzee.

Last month she cut into small pieces Jabari's decoration for valor, which I stupidly left sitting on a low table after I had shown it to her the day before. I had not guessed that she was able to use her little scissors so well, nor that they would cut something that seemed so durable. When I saw the scattering of silk ribbon and golden twine on the table and floor, I felt dizzy and had to sit down. It was just a thing, it was not Jabari, but it was one more bit of him that I will never have again.

I asked Kesi what she had done. She saw the tears in my eyes and knew that something was wrong.

So she said, "Nothing."

I said, "But Baba's ribbon is all cut to bits."

She looked right at it and said, "No, it isn't."

It wasn't a lie, not in the sense that you would mean it. Kesi has learned enough about words to know that they have power. She knows that adults speak of things that are not present in the room, and that these things turn out to be true. It is logical, from her perspective, to think that the words *make* them true. She wished that the ribbon were all in one piece, so she told me, with conviction, that it was. I do not think she expected magic, but rather that the world would conform itself to her words, as (from where she stands) it seems to conform itself to mine.

But at the moment she said it, a miserable voice in my head screamed, *liar*! In that instant I judged her, found her untrustworthy, unloving, selfish. I hated her, and not for the first time.

Then I returned to myself and saw a scared, sad little girl who had not understood what she had done. I took her into my arms and we cried into each other's shoulders.

And I wondered whether someday I will misplace the reason to forgive her — whether there will come an instant of hatred that does not fade.

♎

The war broke out a year after Jabari and I were married. Although trained as a linguist and translator, I elected for combat duty so that we could be posted together. It amazes me that we were not both killed during those first weeks, so complete were the losses at the hands of the Sheshash fighting pairs. Jabari and I fought together in the same unit, one covering for the other in combat, sharing a tent or quarters to ourselves. I do not know how many times he saved my life or I his. Our lovemaking in those days was fierce, desperate and joyful; death hovered near us, and we kept it away by grabbing great fistfuls of life.

When I became pregnant, I was ordered back to non-combatant duty. Our armies still will not allow women with child to fight, and with this Jabari agreed. So I worked on trying to decode the Sheshash language. Jabari also had desk duty for a time, and he was present when our daughter was born.

Then he had the opportunity to go back to combat. Over this decision we had bitter arguments, because he wished me to stay behind again. "I don't want our daughter raised by strangers," he said.

"Then why don't *you* stay behind?"

"Because you can contribute to the war here, and I can't. At a desk I'm useless; I'll rust if I don't go back."

In the end I gave in, though I was sulking when I did it. I saw him only twice again before Heraclea. Some part of me believed, still believes, that if I had been there, I would have seen the danger coming; I would have saved him.

♎

With so little in common besides the war, it was hard to know where to start. But the Sheshash had space travel, which meant they understood physics, therefore mathematics.

I reached into my bag. The giant Sheshash's eyes widened for a moment, then half-closed again when what I drew out was not a weapon.

I held up a white plastic sphere. "Sphere," I said.

The Sheshash regarded me for a while. I did not really expect a response; we'd never had one in the past. Then she said, "*Itto.*"

I hid my surprise at getting a response. The dwarf Sheshash launched itself at the barrier again, and in that instant I felt like a traitor even for trying to talk to the giant. The mother was a liar, the daughter was a killer, these things had killed Jabari, they would kill me.

The giant ignored the dwarf, still looking at me. I looked at her. Then I replaced the sphere and held up a cube, the same color. "Cube," I said.

"*Itto,*" said the giant again.

Very well then, *itto* probably was not "sphere" — unless, to the Sheshash, a sphere and a cube were the same thing. That would be fascinating, but daunting.

I brought up a blue sphere. "Blue," I said.

"*Itto,*" she repeated.

Perhaps it meant "plastic," or "opaque." I lowered the sphere into the bag —

"*Ushata,*" said the Sheshash.

I stopped. Then I slowly raised the sphere. "*Itto*?" I asked. I worried that the rising pitch at the end of the word might signify a wholly different meaning.

"*Itto,*" she agreed.

Then I lowered the sphere again. "*Ushata*?"

"*Ushata.*"

Itto was either a verb, meaning to raise or take out, or an adjective, meaning a higher elevation, or possibly exposure to the elements. A few more experiments persuaded me that it was the verb. *Itto* was "raise," *ushata* was "lower."

Or the whole thing might be a deception. She was, after all, a prisoner in enemy hands. We had treated her and her daughter gently after capture on Asculum, but we could not be sure that "gently" meant the same thing to us as to them, and, in any case, the capture itself must have been brutal.

Still it was a breakthrough, even if she was trying to mislead me.

When I look at Kesi, it is easy to imagine I am seeing a smaller, simpler, more naïve version of myself. I fancy that I remember being her age, can relive the games I played and feel the way she is feeling as she plays now. When she disobeys or defies me, I tell myself that she is just like her mother, that I understand her. This is the life-giving self-deception, like the stories we tell of fierce, protective mothers who die for their young.

A few days ago, the teacher at the preschool called me aside before I picked Kesi up, explaining that there had been "a little incident" and that she had a cut on her forehead. One of the other children, a boy named Edmund, had struck her with a wooden toy. It seems he was playing a game in which he was a soldier and the other children were Sheshash. They had taken Edmund aside and explained what he had done while Kesi cried into the teacher's shirt, then Edmund apologized and helped Kesi clean and bandage the cut.

When I went in, Kesi ran to me and showed off her bandage like a medal.

"Does it hurt?" I asked.

"No. I was Sheshash! He can't hurt me!"

I shuddered inside, but smiled and nodded to her.

As we walked out the door, I tried to decide whether I was more surprised that a little, innocent child could hurt someone, or that human children were civilized at all, and did not simply rip one another's throats out.

I learned to call the mother Ishish, the daughter Ashashi. Without other Sheshash present, I could not know whether *Ishish* was the mother's name, or whether it meant "mother" or simply "adult." It might have some other meaning altogether; it might mean someone who does a certain thing, or even the word for the action itself, although this seemed less likely as time went on.

By now I was consistently thinking of them as mother and daughter. Levi was still skeptical, but the behavioral evidence supported my intuition. Ishish was visibly nurturing, teaching, protecting Ashashi — I could see her modeling behavior which Ashashi then copied, slowing down her speech when Ashashi did not understand the first time, taking Ashashi into her pouch when the child became agitated. Such behavior might be typical for a fighting pair regardless of their relationship, as Levi kept pointing out. But I was sure.

They learned to say my name, after a fashion. Although I'd heard them employing something like our glottal stops, they seemed to have no glottal fricatives, voiced or otherwise, nor voiced alveolars, nor nasal consonants of any kind. (Of course it is misleading to use these terms, which refer to the part of the mouth where speech is made. They have no nasal consonants because they have only one respiratory orifice.) Thus my name Halima became "Atipa." At the time I did not know whether they meant to describe me personally by that name, or female humans, or interrogators.

Beyond my name, they showed no interest in learning our speech, which was just as well; they could not pronounce most of it. I, on the other hand, began to pick up a few dozen words of the Sheshash language.

Most of the attempts at communication I made over the next two weeks were with Ishish. For days after Ishish began speaking to me, Ashashi consistently tried various ways of killing me. Too, Ashasi's use of their language was more rudimentary and less nuanced, and her responses to Ishish were either echoes, queries, or possibly jokes.

But one afternoon, repeatedly distracted from my work by a buzzing fly (Maintenance has never succeeded in eradicating the things), I swatted it on the table without thinking.

Ishish and Ashashi both stopped what they were doing and stared at me for a long moment. I stared back, wondering whether I had committed some sort of transgression.

Then Ashashi said, "*Kri'ikshi akdash kri'ikshi*!" Ishish waited another moment, then confirmed it more calmly: "*Kri'ikshi akdash kri'ikshi.*" *Kri'ikshi*, I had inferred, was the word they used to refer to humans, but it was also their battle cry. Perhaps it meant "enemy?"

For the first time, Ashashi approached me slowly, turning so that each of her eyes could look at me in turn.

Ashashi's attitude changed from that moment. Not only did she begin speaking to me, she spoke nonstop. Most of her sentences were simple, and most of them I could not understand. Like a toddler, she seemed to like showing me the obvious. She would hold up an object and tell me what it was, perhaps copying my own actions, or she would do something and describe it (the way a youngster might say, "Look at me!"). She pointed out Ishish to me frequently, or would say, "Ashashi *shi*" when she crawled into Ishish's pouch.

Ishish seemed interested in getting through to me, although she was selective in the topics she would discuss. Human civilization, human concerns, anything about human beings interested her not at all, except for that single, dismissive term, *kri'ikshi*.

She talked preferentially about Ashashi: what she was doing or learning. Often she would describe Ashashi's actions as Ashashi performed them; I thought she was speaking to me, although possibly she narrated Ashashi's behavior the way parents narrate their children's actions, to teach them the connection between actions and words. As I might say, "Now Kesi picks up the ball," Ishish would say, "Ashashi *akpa'atkoko*," which seemed to mean, "Ashashi is spinning around when she doesn't need to."

Ashashi's greater tendency towards violence, so far as I could tell, seemed natural to Ishish. I wondered, are Sheshash children this brutal on their homeworld, against each other? If so, it's a wonder they survive to adulthood.

Kesi had a tantrum today, a bad one. She was still playing the Sheshash game Edmund had started with her, strutting around the main room of our quarters, making shrieking noises and spinning around, grabbing dolls or toy animals and pretending to kill them. Occasionally she would fall down on the carpet from dizziness, laugh, and start over. It was the sort of game that was amusing at first (if not for the subject matter) but eventually would have set any parent's teeth on edge. As it was, I bit my lip for the last ten minutes, trying to think of a way to distract her without making it obvious how much the game upset me.

I had been trying to ignore her for a while, staring at my work screen and hoping that she would get bored, when I sensed a change. I spun back, and saw that she had climbed up to the table and taken Jabari's framed picture into her pudgy hand. Now she shook it, yelling at her father's image, "You fight Sheshash! You die!"

Before I could even think, I had risen, crossed the room, snatched the photo out of her hand and shouted, "No, Kesi!"

It startled her, but she glared at me. "Give to Sheshash! Sheshash kill!"

I shook my head, not trusting myself to speak, and put the picture on a high shelf. She shouted, "Give me picture!"

"No," I said, as calmly as I could.

"Give! Give! Give, give, give, *give*!"

Then she was on the floor, kicking the legs of the table, banging her fists, yelling so loudly that it seemed her vocal cords would snap. I have learned how to handle such things: I returned to my chair and sat down, although I was shaking. Eventually, I knew, she would tire and calm down, and then I could cuddle her and assure her that I loved her, and we could forget the whole thing.

It took twenty minutes. By the time she was done, face slick with tears and mucous, she was exhausted. I barely had time to take her into my lap before she fell asleep. I did not manage to say "Mzazi loves Kesi" when she could still hear me.

♎

One day, Ishish and Ashashi were both unusually quiet. They answered my questions briefly but did not elaborate. Ashashi moved around the room, but without what I had come to think of as her puppy-like enthusiasm. Eventually she crawled into Ishish's pouch, and said, "*Shi*"—sleep. But she did not sleep; she turned restlessly in the pouch, sticking out one arm at a time. I wondered whether Ashashi was growing too large for the pouch, whether Ishish would have to exile her.

Another fly appeared, this time on Ishish's side of the barrier (a much bigger Maintenance infraction, as the Sheshash were supposed to be in a sealed environment). Ishish saw it, said "*Kri'ikshi*," and whipped out one of her flexible arms; the insect shattered.

Ashashi stirred in Ishish's pouch.

I saw spots when I understood. *Kri'ikshi* didn't mean "human." It meant "pest," "vermin." They didn't see us as opponents in a struggle; they saw us as parasites.

Once this was clear, I was able to ask questions I'd never thought to raise. Ishish spoke about *kri'ikshi*, and about the cell in which she and Ashashi were confined.

On the one hand, *kri'ikshi* (humans) had built the cell, captured and forced them to live there. On the other hand, the cell provided *ata'ashkit*—isolation, solitude, protection, safety. Specifically, it was nearly devoid of *kri'ikshi* (parasites and pathogens, like the fly). She repeated this over and over: *kri'ikshi* built the cell, but the cell kept *kri'ikshi* out. It seemed a paradox to her.

I felt that we had hit the key point, that we were on the verge of a breakthrough. I made Ishish repeat that *kri'ikshi* had built the cell, and that it kept *kri'ikshi* out.

Then I asked, "Halima *atko kri'ikshi*?" I held my breath waiting for the answer.

Finally she said very quietly, "Atipa *sha'etish kri'ikshi*."

Halima is not vermin, not a parasite, not the enemy.

I was halfway to the main entrance when the alarm sounded like a screaming child, hammering the eardrums twice a second until I thought my head would explode.

I phoned Levi as he was about to phone me. "The Sheshash broke out," he said. "They've killed at least six soldiers already and are heading your way."

How Ishish and Ashashi escaped is not important to relate. Our technology perplexes the Sheshash as theirs perplexes us. It may simply have taken Ishish this long to realize that what we thought was an impregnable chamber was as easy to violate as air.

I checked my weapon as I ran back; it was fully charged. I had not fired it in four years outside of mandatory practice, but at that second I did not know whether Ishish would kill me when she saw me, or let me talk to her.

I rounded the corner more quickly than I should have, failing to take the precautions drilled into me. Ishish and Ashashi were at the far end of the corridor, moving so rapidly it was hard to see them, a leapfrogging, swirling gait that made me nauseous. I stopped in my tracks.

"Ishish!" I called.

They stopped immediately, at the same instant, Ashashi a few yards closer to me than Ishish, their arms quivering, their fingers fluttering, their eyes open for battle.

Then, as I watched, their eyes half closed and their limbs slowed.

It was Ashashi who spoke. "Atipa!" Then she turned to her mother. "Atipa *etish kri'ikshi*? *Akdash* Atipa?" Is Halima a parasite, an enemy? Shall we kill her?

Ishish looked at me. "Atipa *sha'etish kri'ikshi. Sha'akdash* Atipa."

Ashashi sidled closer to her mother. "*Sha'etish kri'ikshi*," she repeated.

I lowered my weapon and began to step towards them, realizing that the alarm was no longer sounding, and that I could not remember when it had stopped. I was trying to work out how to get Ishish and Ashashi back to their cell, or to someplace safe, when I heard the pounding footsteps of a dozen sprinting soldiers echoing in the corridor behind me.

What happened next took less than two seconds. I turned back, away from Ishish and Ashashi, getting ready to explain the situation. A lone soldier, who either started from a different location than the others or had got ahead of them, rounded the corner first, his weapon out. He saw the Sheshash the instant I saw him.

I had begun to shout "Stand down!" when he fired.

"No!" I turned back. Ishish was down, a smoldering hole in her. Ashashi was already moving, a greenish-white blur who passed me before I could turn my head again.

When I did look back, the soldier was in two pieces, severed at the chest. Ashashi revolved around the body, screeching "*Kri'ikshi! Kri'ikshi*! Ishish! Ishish!" Her eyes were moving side-to-side.

The other sprinting footsteps came closer; any moment they would be in view.

"Ashashi," I said, wanting to tell this child, this baby, that it was all right, that she could still survive, even without her mother, even as a prisoner in the hands of her enemies.

But she said, "*Kri'ikshi*!" — not towards me; she *trusted* me — but towards the coming footsteps. Another fraction of a second and she would be all over them, a blur of grief and rage that would not stop.

I fired my weapon. The baby popped like a balloon.

♎

I hold Kesi on my lap and stroke her hair, singing lullabies and trying to believe that I love her. She is innocent, she bears no guilt for Jabari's death, for Ashashi's murder. She is a child of war, but she is my child. I should love her. I am sure that I did.

But how am I to love her? As a mother loves? Does a mother kill children? It does no good to tell myself that I probably saved a dozen lives, that Ashashi was the enemy. It does no good to tell myself, "There are no true innocents among the Sheshash; those children kill hundreds."

A child who kills is still a child. A child who kills from grief is even more a child.

In my dreams, sometimes it is Kesi who explodes and crumples. It is Kesi who looks into my eyes and says, "Halima *sha'etish kri'ikshi*." Halima is not the enemy. And then I kill my daughter. And then I wake up.

But I continue to stroke Kesi's hair, I continue to sing. Our children do not know our hearts; they only know what we show them. I will show Kesi the face of a loving mother, whether or not I am one. I will give her what she needs to grow, to thrive, maybe even to trust.

But she should not trust me.

As part of a Kickstarter campaign, I invited story prompts from my backers. Cinthea Stahl, a screenwriter who is too clever by half, provided this one: Marsupials are fierce warriors.

The first draft of the story was called "The Sacred Band", and focused more on the alien Sheshash. But by the time it got to my writer's group, it was clear that the core of the story was parenthood, the alienness of children, and the difficulty of unconditional love. That theme, combined with what Alex Jablokov called the "army composed of Mommy & Me play groups", allowed me to juxtapose the horror of child soldiers with the limitations all parents feel in raising the young.

— KLS

III

The Law & the Heart

The Tortoise Parliament

Although for different reasons, my mistress and I agreed that I should leave her before daybreak in order to return home to my wife. Before I threw off the colorless sheets, Merro grasped me in a fierce, muscular embrace, so that I felt every hair on her body. I think her people are hairier than mine, as well as shorter, and they have no depilatory practices apart from cropping the black hair on their heads. To Merro, my own fastidious hairlessness, the common thing on Olympia where I was born, was a little scandalous, as if she were fornicating with a boy.

She often held me thus, but this morning I thought I felt a new intensity, even desperation. I asked, "What is it?"

She rolled away as if going back to sleep. "Never mind, Tithonos," came her lucid, bitter voice. "I'm just worried about the transport standards."

"I think the Committee will — "

She interrupted me. "No need. Go home."

It was understood that I was not to intrude into her concerns. I might share her bed, but Merro set limits on what else I might share. I had always thought that these rules suited me, but on this particular morning I found that I wanted to know more of her thoughts. I did not ask.

Merro never called herself my *mistress*; it is not a word her people understand. In the language of Kern, the closest synonym is *thief*. Discovery by those who sent her to Bower would mean revocation of her commission and disgrace, at least in theory. In practice, it would take some thirty-nine standard years for news of an infraction to reach the Designee of Kern. By then, Merro's replacement would already have arrived; presumably the Designee sent her relief while she was still in transit, as mine left Olympia before I arrived. Still, to her the risk of shame was real.

Our liaison began two years before, while we served together on the Subcommittee on Precious Metals. Kern mines gold, cobalt and silver, while Olympia, lacking easy access to these elements, fashions sculptures from them, so that our legislative interests were technically adverse. But as was often the case in the Parliament of the Confederation of Inhabited Worlds (the "Tortoise Parliament," as Merro called it without humor), we discovered much common ground when we began to discuss points of policy. We would sit later than the other delegates in the sumptuous committee workroom, sometimes long into the evening.

We had a cultural misunderstanding. Merro's burning stare I took for erotic curiosity, while she thought my polite compliments of her face and voice were attempts at seduction. It irritated her, which increased the beautiful ferocity of her gaze, which prompted me to compliment her more frequently — an ascending spiral, dizzy and unsteady. Then one night she rose, said "I can't stand this," pulled me out of my chair, and kissed me.

I know now that she was angry with herself. The hunger of her body offended her; her loneliness she saw as weakness.

This morning, as on so many others, I needed to get home ahead of the tentative proposal of dawn to be in my own room with my wife Psamathe before we showed our public faces. She naturally expected me to exercise good taste and not make a spectacle of myself. An Olympian would no more announce having a mistress or paramour than introduce his servants to guests.

Psamathe was already dressing when I pulled open the heavy, polished door of our bedroom. She hooked an elbow around my neck and kissed me playfully. We were exactly the same height, the same coloring; her dark yellow braid nearly matched her gleaming scalp.

"How is your little mistress?" she asked.

"Well, thank you."

"Did she teach you any new tricks last night?" Psamathe lifted her razor-thin eyebrows and grinned.

"No, none to speak of."

"Tsk, what a shame. If you are free to stay with me tonight." She held a fingertip against my chest. "I might show you some new tricks of my own." Psamathe's paramour was inventive, as she was always telling me.

"Of course."

"Good." She tapped the finger on my chest. "What are your obligations today?"

"Annika debates the genome question until noon. In the afternoon, the Committee on Transport Standards."

"Hmm, that's the bill about Kern, isn't it?"

"Yes." Kern closely orbits an orange dwarf star, vulnerable to any stellar fits or tantrums. They had been experiencing increased solar flare activity for decades. It had impacted their climate, slowing down their mining and other industries and causing them to miss deadlines and quotas on deliveries of ore and refined metals. These lapses had become so numerous and severe that the Parliament was considering legislation on sanctions for chronically unreliable deliveries — a provision that would, in practice, apply only to Kern. Hence Merro's worries about the Transport Standards negotiations.

Psamathe said, "And I shall languish here, writing yet another dull paper on neomonetarist trade theory."

"The same paper, I believe."

She pinched me. "Don't forget: this evening we have the reception for Orlando's anniversary."

"His fifteenth, yes?"

"Yes."

"I shall wear silk."

♎

The whimsical designers who planned the Parliament's campus, three hundred years ago, modeled it on the sort of archaic-Terra university that once trained clergymen and the sons of the mighty. We lived in red-brick houses with octagonal towers and tall, narrow windows, an easy walk from the meeting rooms, social gathering places, and the Parliament chamber itself. In the warm breeze, I listened to the unhurried scrapes and faint echoes of my footsteps on the flagstones.

I ascended the wide, stone staircase into the Chamber. It resembled a medieval banquet hall: stone floor with thick rugs, enormous windows graced with stained-glass insets depicting great events from the history of the Confederation. The acoustics were terrible.

Inside, about twenty delegates already sat — not nearly enough for a quorum, had a quorum been required. The desks formed a crescent seven rows deep, so that all could see the delegate speaking from the rostrum. At the moment, it was empty; the Speaker sat at her own desk to the left of the rostrum, engaged in a lively conversation with Yitzakh of Tikkun. Everyone chatted with friends and colleagues except for Annika of Himmel, who was perusing the text of her speech, and Merro, who sat alone.

Annika, tall even when seated, pale and thin with a dark-green rune tattooed on her forehead, wore not the undyed, natural fibers that the Himmelli display with such relish, but the pastel cotsilk robes that were popular at the Parliament. We had each arrived on Bower wearing our native garb, the most status-conscious we could find, but within a year or two, nearly everyone sported the cotsilks. They were well-adapted to the climate, but, more important, when one spends every day for twenty years with the same people, it feels natural to blend in with them. Of all of us, Merro wore the cotsilks least often, but not in favor of the bright colors that would have shown off her black hair and eyes. Instead she preferred the dark, heavy working garb of Kern. She was wearing such an outfit this day: a coverall of brown denim with a badge of office on the shoulder.

Annika was one of Merro's few friends at Parliament, quick and mischievous where Merro was intense and grave. They attended each other's speeches like supporters at an athletic contest. Annika's presentation today was part of the twenty-fourth debate on the definition of "person" for purposes of reciprocity of citizenship.

Just before the address, Orlando of Halcyon bustled apologetically into the hall. A stout, dark-skinned, grey-bearded man, Orlando looked absurd in the cotsilks. He bowed to the Speaker, sat down on his chair — and shot up again with a yelp. He glared at Annika, who did not return his glance but smirked as she looked over her notes. Orlando snatched the tickler disk off his chair and stuffed it into his bag, then sat again, fuming.

I sometimes wondered whether playing pranks is a customary pastime among the Himmelli or a quirk of Annika alone. Most of us made a habit of checking our chairs and desks.

"The question of boundaries," Annika began, her strong, low voice reverberating on the bare walls and ceiling, "is inherently fluid in the absence of natural separations. On the one hand, any genome will invariably have variations, so that clear delineation of a 'species' is suspect. At one time . . ."

We had heard similar arguments before; I could have written out a fair approximation of the speech myself. But an article of faith at the Parliament was that an issue should be addressed repeatedly, in detail, and with the greatest possible nuance, before any action was taken. This followed naturally from the fact that none of us received instructions from home any sooner than a decade, sometimes a century, after they were sent. We all knew that we were working from obsolete information, and that our decisions, if they were to serve any purpose at all, must remain relevant in all climates. Slow deliberation seemed the best course. It was even written into the Charter.

Three hours later, after the customary applause, Merro walked over and put her hand on Annika's arm, speaking softly. The taller woman bowed her head and murmured into Merro's ear, one corner of her mouth twitching. Merro rolled her eyes and gave a little *huff*, then shook her head and strode away.

I fell in step beside Merro. She always took energetic, decisive strides, as if finding the quickest way out of an unpleasant place.

"What were you saying to Annika?" I asked.

"That she wastes our time. That she says nothing that hasn't been said in earlier presentations."

"I can imagine what she said to that."

Merro rolled her eyes again. "She said that one doesn't criticize a dancer by saying she didn't reach the other side of the floor in the most efficient way."

"She has a point."

Merro's hands flicked up in a gesture of impatience. "But she isn't a dancer. This isn't a performance."

"Are we in a hurry to reach a resolution on this issue? It is a pleasure to see Annika's work."

"We're never in a hurry about anything," said Merro. "Nobody wants to reach any conclusions."

Impatient as Merro could be with our process, it was unusual for her to express irritation with Annika. I said, "Is there something else?"

Her mouth tightened, and I expected her to shut me out again. But then she said, "I'm expecting a report from home tomorrow, about the solar flares."

A report *tomorrow* meant a report sent nearly forty years before. Bad as Kern's trade situation was, the consequences of the flares could be far worse. I asked, "Has there been damage?"

She shook her head. "The last communiqué said that the Astrophysical College expected to make an announcement. It's overdue."

Of course she was fretting. I was touched that she'd told me. "Is there anything I can do?"

"No." Then, in a lower, if not a softer tone: "No, thank you, Tithonos. The news will be what it will be."

We approached the stone fountain where our paths would separate — I toward the workroom for my committee, she for home. I remembered what I needed to tell her.

"Psamathe wishes me to stay at home tonight."

Merro bent slightly at the waist, continuing her pace but looking down at the foot of the fountain. "Of course." Her posture displayed not the sullenness of a jealous lover, but the resignation of a fugitive. A pang twisted the space behind my eyes, and I felt like a callous idiot for choosing that moment to mention it.

Not for the first time, I thought of breaking off the affair for her sake. Olympian courtesy does not sanction a dalliance when it becomes more than a convenient pastime. Kernish mores do not permit it at all. It was hurting her.

But I could not say the words. I told myself that the timing was wrong, that this was a cruel moment to trouble her about such things. But the truth, the truth I would not admit, was that her grim countenance and flat, truthful voice had become necessary to me, like an anchor. I feared losing her.

♎

It might seem surprising that such influential delegates as Annika and Yitzakh served on so minor a committee as Transport Standards. But it was responsible for the report on the proposed punitive measures against Kern, and I had suggested to them that they could do some mundane legislative labor to show the junior delegates that they shared the burdens. Orlando and Dzuling of Tianming welcomed us newcomers to the Committee and pretended not to notice if we had our own agenda.

I even served as Vice Chair, and this day I was to run the meeting, as Dzuling was having her annual attack of allergies to the flora of Bower.

A tart, fragrant luncheon was served by Dzuling's favorite cuisinartists, and we gossiped over our meal before coming to order.

"Today we review the fifth draft of the Report on Anomalous Interworld Orders and Deliveries," I said. "Yitzakh has done a masterful job, I think all will agree."

"Yitzakh is always masterful," said Annika.

Yitzakh snorted and waved a hand at her for silence. "Anything I've done is the result of Tithonos's excellent first draft, Dzuling's superb second draft, Annika's *masterful* third draft —

"Very well," I said. "First of all, has anyone received any — "

Yitzakh and Annika finished in chorus: " — *new instructions from home?*" Everyone laughed. Protocol required that I put the question, but the concept of *new* instructions was so absurd that one could not recite it without irony.

"Have the vague terms concerning nonconforming tender been resolved to everyone's satisfaction?"

There was a moment of silence while everyone reread those paragraphs.

"Well," said Orlando. "I suppose that the term 'machine' could be better defined — "

Annika groaned. "Sun and rain, Orlando! Every single time. Nitpicking perfectionist, I wonder how Miranda lives with you. Why don't *you* volunteer for the next draft?"

Orlando beamed at her. "I should do that, if only as repayment for the tickler disk, you adolescent. However, I can live with the current imperfections, for Yitzakh's sake."

"Don't do me any favors," said Yitzakh.

"Dear man," said Orlando, reaching over and patting Yitzakh's hand. "Your work is splendid, as always. I'm sure you'd show me the same consideration if our places were reversed."

"Certainly."

"Well, then."

There was a pause. I asked, "Is everyone still comfortable with the current language on timeliness of off-world requests?" A general murmur of assent followed. "Do we want to proceed to a final report to the full Parliament, without further discussion or drafts?"

Annika pointed out, "Article 17, Section 4(d) of the Charter requires seven drafts under normal circumstances." Only Annika could quote the precise subsection, a talent about which she was unbearably smug. A few people sighed; they were tired of this document, but there was no basis on which we could find "abnormal" circumstances to shorten the process.

"Annika should do the next draft, as punishment," said Orlando.

"Punishment for quoting the Charter, or for the tickler disk?" she asked.

"Both."

"No, Wise Delegate of Halcyon; I already did one. Your turn. Happy anniversary."

I asked, "Is there an objection to Orlando's preparation of the sixth draft?"

"Apart from mine?" growled Orlando.

"Out of order. We will reconvene in four standard months, to examine Orlando's sixth draft."

Things were well in hand. The negotiations so far had given every appearance of calm give-and-take between worlds with disparate interests, but Dzuling, Annika, Yitzakh and I had contrived to word the document so that circumstances warranting sanctions would never coincide with sanctions of any consequence. Orlando, who saw what we were doing, would go along for the sake of earning later favors from us, and because he enjoyed process without conflict.

Merro would never have countenanced such a backhanded way of protecting her planet. She would have preferred an open, honest fight — which she would have lost. One does for one's friends what they cannot do for themselves.

Annika loved the ploy's cunning; Yitzakh appreciated the precision and misdirection of the wording; Dzuling simply disliked having her committee used for a vendetta against one world. As for me, although Olympia had never given explicit instructions on the topic, I knew that our Council of Arbiters frowned on Confederation intervention in private commerce; this was the justification I mentioned aloud. But in truth, I had dreams about the miners of Kern, plagued by a wrathful sun, suffering wrong upon wrong as the Parliament penalized them for something they could not control.

They all had Merro's face.

♎

When I returned home to dress for Orlando's reception, waiting for me like a bad joke was the first official message I had received in three years from Olympia. It had been sent some 28 years earlier, while I was still on my way to Bower to assume my post.

> Delays and substandard shipments from Kern have resulted in steadily increasing costs for replacement materials and lost opportunities for sales. Much as we sympathize with the plight of Kern, Olympian vital interests will best be served by imposing greater discipline on our trading partners. If Confederation policies are proposed to levy sanctions against worlds dishonoring good-faith agreements, you are directed to support such measures.
>
> We realize that by the time you receive this directive, you will have been working diligently for more than twelve standard years to advocate Olympia's prior trade policies. We feel confident that you will find a way to effectuate our developing economic priorities.
>
> Cytherea, Lead Arbiter (for the Council)

I stood still, my mouth open, trying to imagine what Orlando would say when I told him, to say nothing of Annika. Merro's reaction I did not want to think about.

Psamathe, who had stolen into the room as I read, put her hand on my shoulder. She nodded slowly while reading the new directive, pursing her lips and narrowing her eyes as she did when thinking hard. Finally she looked up. "Well, this was coming. I told them as much in my last presentation to the Council before we left."

"Well, yes, but — " I spluttered, hardly knowing where to begin. "But the last five drafts of the Report have been anchored on the importance of nonintervention! Every word I have written, not to mention every speech in the Chamber, has been based on that principle. I will look like a fool. And how will I ever persuade the others to reverse course on such a fundamental issue?"

My wife considered for a moment, tilting her head to look at the message from a different angle. "With two more drafts to go, and three years before a vote on the legislation, a subtle, mm, nudge at this point could be enough to deflect the trajectory in a more, mm, *congenial* direction." Her voice had become playful; Psamathe could make political strategy seem like a game of seduction.

"Perhaps," I said, trying not to be distracted as her hand snaked around my waist. "But I'm not sure that it would be the best thing to do."

Her hand stopped sliding, and she pulled away to look at me. "How do you mean?"

"Well, think of how many years members have been working on this bill in good faith. It seems unfair to Dzuling, Yitzakh, and the others to *nudge* them abruptly in another direction, as if Olympia's interests trumped everyone else's."

She frowned as she settled herself on the divan near the door. "You represent Olympia, not Tienming or Tikkun, and you certainly don't represent Dzuling or Yitzakh. It isn't about them personally."

"I am not so certain of that," I said. I sat down next to her and put my hand on her knee, but she slid away — not very far away, though. "No one at home understands the daily reality of working in the Parliament for ten or twenty years. All we have are our families here and the others who have devoted their lives to it. Besides, what am I here for, if not to see the big picture?"

She slid back to me so that her leg touched mine. "How can there be a big picture without the little pieces — " she walked her fingers from my knee to my thigh " — that make it up? If you don't speak in Olympia's voice, no one will. Do you suppose that the others sacrifice their planets' interests for the sake of the big picture?" Her fingers were now walking up my side toward my armpit.

A vision of Merro's face came into my mind. "Merro probably doesn't," I admitted.

"*Yes*," said Psamathe, now running her fingers through my hair. "Tell me more about *Merro*. Does she like to nibble and bite? Does she swallow you whole? Does she ride you like a horsemistress, bucking to stay in the saddle?" Nothing aroused Psamathe more quickly than to hear me speak of my mistress; she began to nip at my neck, and with one foot she shut the door of the study. I should have enjoyed this game too, talking of Merro as if she were a toy we shared.

"She — " Unseemly it might be, but I felt reluctant to satisfy Psamathe's curiosity; I told myself that Merro's performance would disappoint her. "She holds on very tight. Her arms and legs are strong, and she wraps me in them and will not let go."

"Ah, a struggle," she said, hooking my elbow and pulling it around my back. "I can offer you a struggle too." She chuckled and began to search for the fastenings of my robe. "Prepare to do battle for the sweetest of all prizes."

"We will be late for the reception," I said.

"Unquestionably," she purred. "They will all know exactly what we have been doing."

Psamathe's playful, competitive eroticism was a window into her complex, subtle mind, so very different from Merro's. In five years, Merro had avoided the socializing and friendships that made the members of Parliament seem more real than the remnants of family and friends at home. Except with a few of us, like Annika and Yitzakh. Except with me.

What I did not say to my wife was that Merro's intensity in bed was not about struggle. She clung to me with helpless, desperate longing, with hungry eyes that spoke of a starving soul. Now I began to fear what Merro might see revealed in my own eyes.

♎

Every delegate and spouse was present in the echoing, torch-lit ballroom, as were many of their children. Even Dzuling had appeared, looking woozy and leaning on one of her wives to keep from falling over.

Yitzakh, dressed in one of the shiny black suits he wears only at the most festive events, was entertaining the spouses of five delegates with his favorite parlor trick. Both an accomplished polyglot and a gifted storyteller, he regaled them with a long, outrageous tale, shifting from one of their native languages to another, then to Lingua Franca, then to his own strange tongue and back again.

After giving Orlando my congratulations, I contrived to steer him away from the punch bowl long enough to tell him of the communiqué from Olympia.

He looked appalled. "You're joking."

"No. They direct a complete reversal."

He took a long drink of punch, then belched silently. "Twenty-eight years. I wonder if they still feel the same way now."

"The same thought had occurred to me."

He held his breath for a moment, released it, then raised the spicy cup of punch to his lips but did not drink.

Slowly he asked, "Do you want me to try to write the sixth draft along those lines?"

I shook my head. "If I begin taking a hard line on Olympian interests, you can depend on Annika and Yitzakh to do the same for Himmel and Tikkun in other committees."

"Not to mention me," said Orlando.

"Not to mention you."

He took my arm and led me back toward the punch; I had not noticed when he finished his cup. "Those fellows on the home worlds," he said. "They have no conception. We are not devices to be turned on and off. It takes years of building trust and loyalty to make a government like ours operate, if it operates at all."

"Yes."

"I wonder . . . " He lowered his voice. "I wonder whether the microwave reception between Olympia and Bower is as reliable as it could be. Messages can be garbled."

"Or lost altogether," I said.

"Just so."

"Orlando? If you would refrain from mentioning this conversation to Psamathe, I would be obliged."

He nodded. He did not wink; on a face like his, it would seem absurd.

Just then, a clerk from Communications came in through the main door. He found Merro and said something in her ear. She nodded, touched Annika's arm, and followed the clerk out.

♎

The butler system had to call several times before I heard; Psamathe didn't wake at all. I blinked to bring the room into focus, untangled myself from her warm, golden limbs, threw on my light wrap, walked down the hallway to the butler system's node, and read the message.

> At the request of Delegate Merro of Kern, an Extraordinary Session of the Parliament of the Confederation of Inhabited Worlds is called for 1000 this morning. The attendance of all Delegates is requested.

I had to read the note three times to understand it. Psamathe appeared as I was finishing breakfast, looking rumpled, soft, and disappointed, and asked what made me rise so early. I told her.

"An Extraordinary Session? When have we had one of those?"

"Never, so far as I know."

"Tithonos," she said, regarding me with her clever eyes. "We gave up twenty years of our lives, and everyone we knew, to serve Olympia. Now, when it matters most, remember it."

The sky had turned grey overnight, and the flagstones were cold. The Chamber was nearly full when I arrived; the light through its stained-glass

windows muted, and the delegates' seats seemed farther apart than the
should. Merro, sitting painfully straight at her own desk across the hal
held her face in a tight mask. I tried to catch her eye, but she did n
respond.

At exactly 1000 she stood, looking frightened. If not for the micropho
pasted to her throat she would have been inaudible, for her voice was
raspy whisper.

"Last night I received a message from the Designee of Kern, sent 39.
standard years ago. The astronomical observations that have puzzled o
astrophysicists for decades have finally been resolved. Our sun is beginnin
a period of brightening and enhanced flare activity that will increa
steadily over the next several centuries. Within 180 years of the date of th
message, less than 140 years from now, it will render the surface of Ke
uninhabitable." Several people gasped. Merro's voice quavered, but her fa
remained fixed, as if cast in bronze.

She continued, "There is no known way to prevent this calamity. Th
forces involved are too large, and the time too short. Our only option
planet-wide evacuation."

A burst of confused chatter began in the hall, but Merro overrode i
"Our world has a population of over 250 million. A strict fertility-contr
plan was ordered just before the message was sent, and the Design
believes that our numbers will be reduced to two hundred million withi
fifty years; but even so, the project is nearly impossible. No more tha
two evacuations to any of the nearest inhabited worlds are feasible in th
time remaining. Conservatively, 200,000 vessels of the largest size will b
required."

Somebody let out a loud "huh!" of surprise. Merro continued.

"Given the limits on our planetary technology and access to the natur
resources in Kern's upper crust, we cannot manufacture and launch mo
than a fraction of that number. We appeal, therefore, to our brothers an
sisters of other worlds. If the thirty-five inhabited planets within eigh
light years of Kern devote themselves to the task, no more than 5,700 shi
will be required from each planet. Our engineers have calculated that it
possible for you to achieve this."

In a violation of protocol, Floran of Viridia interrupted. "Possibl
yes, but barely so. Building 5,700 maximum-capacity ships within, wha
twenty years, would strain Viridia's resources to the breaking point. O
economy would collapse. Chaos and even civil war could follow."

Merro's jaw tightened. "I agree. The Designee sent his plea to the thirty-five worlds at the same time he sent it to us. We anticipate that they will raise the same objection noted by Delegate Floran. Therefore we ask the Parliament to resolve that *all* the Confederated Worlds will aid in this task, that they will transfer resources and wealth to the thirty-five proximate planets to offset the crushing cost of this emergency effort. It will make everyone a little poorer, but a whole people will be saved."

She sat down abruptly, her mouth thin and pale, her hands clasped tightly together.

After a minute of whispering and shifting chairs, the Speaker stood. "According to normal procedure, the matter should be referred to an appropriate subcommittee for the statutory period of deliberation."

Merro shot up again. "Madam Speaker, the statutory period of subcommittee deliberation is two *years*. The periods of full committee consideration and Parliamentary debate are another three years together. We cannot wait! Unless this Parliament acts now, within a year at most, we will fail."

It looked as if the session would decompose into a squabble about procedure. Some argued that the irregularity of her request delegitimized it.

"The Delegate of Himmel," said the Speaker. Annika had risen, and she began to speak in a serious voice that almost hid the mischievous look on her face.

"Madam Speaker, I believe that Article 23, Section 5(b) of the Charter provides for emergency action by the full Parliament."

The Chamber echoed with muttered questions as everyone called up the Charter on his or her desk. The section was exactly as Annika said, but the annotations confirmed that no one had ever invoked it.

She continued, "Under the procedure set out in Section 5(b), I move for the appointment of an ad-hoc committee, to report back to the full Parliament in no more than thirty days."

I seconded the motion. The Speaker consulted the Manual and the Charter and, determining that a full vote was not required for the appointment, said, "The motion is in order. Delegates Merro, Annika — " She saw my raised finger. " — Tithonos and Yitzakh will make up the Committee and report in the allocated period. This extraordinary session is adjourned."

Five minutes later, Annika, Yitzakh, Merro, and I came together at the rostrum. I was about to suggest a timetable, but Annika took my hand and

Merro's and placed them one atop the other. She raised them while bowing her head, until her rune touched Merro's fingers. Then she lowered our hands, said something low and solemn in the nasal language of Himmel, performed a half-pirouette and tripped away.

Yitzakh proposed a meeting time. I waited until Merro left the Chamber, then asked him, "Did you understand that?"

"Certainly. Annika said, *Before love, all things must give way*. It's a fragment of the Himmelli ceremony of betrothal."

For twenty-five days, I did nothing but the work of the ad-hoc committee. Merro's detailed knowledge of Kern, Annika's mastery of precedent and tradition, Yitzakh's delicate touch with language, and my own grasp of the shifting loyalties and rivalries within the Parliament fit together like the pieces of a mosaic. I spent hours consulting the delegates of planets that would be called upon to send ships to the rescue, and from wealthy worlds that would be asked to fund them.

We drafted a bill committing the Confederation as a whole to undertake the evacuation of Kern. The initial investment would amount to a painful six percent of planetary trade revenues for two decades from all worlds not directly involved in the fleet, to be paid as trade credits to the planets building the ships. The extension of credits would begin immediately in order to provide seed capital.

Responses ranged from passionate support to outraged opposition. The Speaker set a period of fifty days in which to deliberate and confer before a vote; only a fraction of the delegates would have the opportunity to speak in unlimited debate, an unheard-of restriction. Without the leisure of a decade in which to evolve a consensus, we found ourselves making unaccustomed appeals to sentiment, vanity, and greed, manipulating our colleagues with a shamelessness that fascinated and appalled us.

Merro became more distant during this time. I shared her bed less often, and when I did, I thought I felt a surge of anger behind the fierceness of her embrace.

Perhaps forty days into the deliberations, I shared a luncheon with Orlando, a meal heavy in the shellfish of which he was especially fond. I took the opportunity to ask his views on the evacuation resolution, about which he had said little.

"No doubt you'll find a way to buy my vote as you've bought so many others," he said with a sour expression.

"Buy your vote? Will I have to?"

"How not? Surely you don't expect me, without bribery, to agree that the whole human universe has to take responsibility for the irresponsible actions of one planet."

"What do you mean?"

"Two hundred and fifty million people, Tithonos. The human population on Kern is only about three centuries old, and there were only five thousand at the start. Do you know what that means? It means that the average Kernish woman in *each generation* has borne five children who survived to adulthood. They breed like rabbits! And then there's the location itself. Technically Kern is a habitable world, but it's circling a K5 star! Any astrophysicist would warn you, and must have warned *them*, about the hazards around such a sun. The planet never had a good supply of building materials near the surface, and the Kerners haven't concentrated on the sorts of industries that would allow them to exploit what they've got. They *put themselves* in this position, and now they're asking us to pull them out of the fire. How many billions, for how many generations, will have their futures wrecked because of this? How many beggars will starve? How many do we trade for them?"

"I do not think such a calculation can be made. They are human."

Orlando shook his heavy head. "Such platitudes are unbecoming and dishonest of you, Tithonos. It's clear why *you* are trying so hard to pass this bill."

"What do you mean?"

"Olympians excel at misdirection and façade, but Kerners wear their hearts on their sleeves. Look who's fighting for the resolution: Annika, Yitzakh, Dzuling, and above all, you. This was never about humanity, never even about Kern. So far as the delegates are concerned, this is all about Merro."

♎

I should have foreseen the outcome. We were accustomed to the "big picture," the interstellar scale, the long view of centuries. Merro's vivid descriptions of the children of Kern, the hardscrabble everyday existence, may have swayed a few, and some were inclined to be generous at the start.

But Orlando was right: nearly all who voted for the rescue did so for love of Merro herself; her people were an abstraction.

Merro's house let me in without challenge. I found her in the solarium, ten thousand crystal panes revealing the comfortable, pampered landscape. She was looking out at the setting sun and the first bright stars. Her face was stone, if stone can bleed.

I put my arms around her from behind. She turned and leaned her forehead on my collarbone, her breathing harsh.

"Not even a close vote," she said at last. "I couldn't even muster a decent fight."

"We couldn't," I said.

"It wasn't your battle."

She stood still, locking her hands at the small of my back and pressing into me. Then she turned her head so that her cheek was against my chest.

"I'm going back," she said.

"What?"

"I'm leaving for Kern, probably within two months."

Nothing moved, but my body felt heavier, while hers felt like air, like water.

She continued, "A ship is due from Bifrost, continuing in the direction of Viridia and Kern. The total trip will only be about sixty years, or two for me."

"You will go back to a doomed planet?"

"It won't be 'doomed' till after I'm dead."

"But why?" I asked.

"Because nothing that I do here, *nothing*, makes any difference. Even physical labor to build the escape ships would be better than this."

I swallowed. I saw three more stars come out.

"I will go with you," I said.

There was a pause. Her cheek still rested against my chest.

"I will go with you," I repeated. "I won't leave you. I will help you in your struggle."

"You won't," she said.

"Yes, I will." I took a deep breath, not knowing what I was going to say until I said it: "I love you."

"No, you *won't*," she said — only it was more of a snarl. Abruptly she pushed against me and broke away, then strode to the other side of the room.

"Merro, I — "

"You *won't*. I won't allow it. Isn't it bad enough that I steal the body of another woman's husband? Now you'd make me the murderer of a family?"

"I love — "

"*Don't* love me," she ordered. "I'm not yours to love. You're not mine..."

I thought I heard a catch in her voice, and stupidly drew encouragement from it. "Merro, I *want* to be yours. I want — "

"I don't care!" She was shouting now. "I won't have it! You cannot shame me like this. Get out."

"What?"

But she turned her back to me, half-ran out of the solarium, and did not return. After a half-hour's silent wait, I returned to Psamathe.

♎

I have spent the last month turning my existence before me in my hands, like an oversized, garish jewel. I have devoted my adulthood, as Psamathe says, to the service of Olympia. But membership in the Parliament does not serve Olympia; realistically it cannot. I would have betrayed any of Olympia's interests for the sake of my colleagues here, and I can think of no one apart from Merro who would have done otherwise. She was right to say that nothing we do here matters.

Then there is Merro herself, and Psamathe. I should have broken off the affair as soon as I realized the shame it caused Merro. Even if I could forgive myself that, Psamathe deserved a husband who would not allow his dalliance to become an embarrassment. When I began to see Merro's face in my dreams, that was the time to end it.

To sum up, then: I have been too foolish to work anywhere but the Parliament, too feckless to do so diligently on behalf of my people, too weak to give my wife her due, and too selfish to honor the needs of the mistress I loved. What remains?

I am going to Kern.

I will not be traveling with Merro, although we will both ride the Bifrost vessel. She has not spoken to me since that night, nor do I expect her to begin.

Psamathe and I sent the registration of our divorce to Olympia a few days ago, along with her consent to replace me as Olympia's Delegate to the Tortoise Parliament. She still believes that Olympia will benefit from the diligence of our Delegate here. I have lost that faith, lost it with each "No" vote answering Merro's plea for help.

I think Psamathe is more shocked, even more hurt, by my betrayal of our world than by my desertion of our marriage. She would have found it insulting had I left her for one of the coarse, hairy Kerners, but she cannot believe that I would leave my post for an abstraction.

Can I be of more use on Kern, among strangers with whom I share nothing, paying out my lifespan on a project that must, in some measure, fail?

Some few worlds will help, planets close enough to build and launch ships to take the children of Kern to safety. But they will be far too few. Others will send token fleets, or devote funds to pay for a tithe of ships, or shrug their shoulders tragically and write long, soul-searching epics about humanity's failure to take care of its own. They will feel exquisitely sad and deliciously guilty, and morally superior for expressing the enormity of their crime with such eloquence.

And I? Am I engaging in another self-indulgent whim, another proof of weakness and fecklessness? I am not qualified to judge. But any small measure of work I can provide — be it only building things with my hands — will be more than what I have accomplished here. It could hardly be less.

Star federations are a silly idea if you take the laws of physics seriously, even if interstellar travel is possible. I tried to imagine what it would be like trying to run such a super-state using near-light, time-dilated transportation and no easy workaround like an "ansible." The more I thought about it, the stranger such a government began to seem.

I didn't realize until the second draft how much of this story was influenced by my feelings about contemporary first-world society and indifference toward the desperate conditions of other nations. Some readers might observe that Tithonos's prediction of "soul-searching epics about humanity's failure to take care of its own" could describe this story. Of course it does.

— KLS

Tenure Track

ROGER WILLIAMS MEDICAL CENTER

Department of Geriatrics

Extended Life Informed Consent Form

Name: *Martin Fournier*

Date: *May 21, 2060*

DOB: *September 24, 2019*

By signing below, you certify that:

1. You have elected the Extended Life Treatment (ELT) voluntarily, under no inducement or offer of compensation from Roger Williams Medical Center (the Hospital) or any of its employees.

2. You understand that, while increased lifespan is the expected outcome of the ELT, this outcome cannot be, and is not, guaranteed by the Hospital.

3. You understand that the benefits of the ELT are reduced when the treatment is begun at a later age. At your age, *40*, the median expected lifespan is *370* years, and the maximum is *408* years.

4. You understand that the ELT is not reversible once it has been performed.

5. You understand that ELT provides no protection against bacteria, viruses, genetic disorders or toxic substances.

6. You understand that side effects are known to occur in a very small number of ELT cases. These include headache, reduced blood pressure, nausea, dizziness, abdominal pain and fatigue. You should not drink alcohol, use aspirin or any prescription medication for a period of 24 hours following the ELT, except at the express direction of your physician.

7. You agree to assume the risks of the ELT described above, and will hold the Hospital, its directors, officers and employees, harmless for any injuries or damages arising out of the treatment.

Signature: *Martin Fournier*

KARA H. ROUGE, BOOKSELLER, LONDON

August 3, 2060

Mrs. Tamara Fournier

27 Whipple Avenue

Barrington, Rhode Island, 02806-30052

United States

tamara.fournier@ridem.gov.us

Dear Mrs. Fournier:

In response to your query, we do have Lord Brabourne's edition of Jane Austen's letters, published by Richard Bentley, London, 1884. It is a first edition, octavo, in two volumes, comprising 374 and 366 pages, respectively, dark green cloth with gilt monogram device, with beveled edges. The set is in very good condition.

We are asking £2,030. In answer to your other question, it is indeed possible to pay this amount in as many as four monthly installments, provided that the first installment is paid before shipping. If we ship within the next seven days, we can guarantee delivery before your husband's birthday.

Cheers,

Kara H. Rouge, Proprietress

RHODE ISLAND PUBLIC TRANSIT AUTHORITY

Receipt for RIPTA Fare Card Purchase

Name: *Martin Fournier*

Date: *9-1-2060*

_2_ Semi-annual card(s) $900.00

Total received: *$1,800.00*

Save this receipt for your records. Fares are 100% tax deductible under both Rhode Island and Federal law.

Don't forget the additional 100% tax credit for proof that you have sold your personal motor vehicle without replacing it. See the U.S. Internal Revenue Svc and the RI Dept of Revenue for Details.

PROVIDENCE COLLEGE

Office of the Provost

May 17, 2061

Martin Fournier

Department of Literature

Dear Prof. Fournier:

I am pleased to inform you that the College Tenure Committee, on the enthusiastic recommendation of your Department, has approved your application for tenure. Effective September 1, you will hold the rank of Associate Professor.

Congratulations on your achievement.

Sincerely,

Hannah G. Laski

Provost

♎

HAW THEATRE FESTIVAL

iagara-on-the-Lake, Ontario

)65 Season Reservation Form

___Threepenny Opera

___Mrs. Warren's Profession

___Saint Joan

___Importance of Being Earnest

___How I Learned to Drive

___Misdirected Love

___Persuasion

___Sense and Sensibility

___Emma

_2_Jane Austen Special Package (all three Austen plays!)

ame: *Martin and Tamara Fournier*

referred dates: *August 2-8*

otal Price: $1,200 CAN

♎

/ISHING WELL FARM

o-Op Organic Produce Subscription Renewal for 2068

ame: *Tamara and Martin Fournier*

gn me up for:

_X_Complete package (full access to all produce with draw-down amounts through October 31), Barrington site, Wednesday afternoons: $2,100

___Complete package (full access to all produce with draw-down amounts through October 31), Providence site, Saturday mornings: $2,100

_X_Reduce your price by $400 by volunteering at Wishing Stone Farm.

I will work:

___At the farm itself. (Sunday afternoons)

_X_At the Barrington site.

___At the Providence Site.

Remember to complete your subscription (including payment!) by April 30th.

♎

ROGER WILLIAMS MEDICAL CENTER

Blood Chemistry Report

Patient Name: *Tamara Fournier*

DOB: *January 4, 2021*

Time Since Patient's Last Meal: *12+ hours*

Time Since Patient's Last Alcohol/Aspirin: *12+ hours*

Date/Time Specimen Collected: *May 21, 2070, 9:38 a.m.*

Glucose: *94* (normal: 67-99 mg/dl)

Cholesterol: *210* (40+ years: low risk if <240)

Extended Life Markers: *1.2 k/μl* (ELR normal: 150-220 k/μl)

Comment: *Chemistry is consistent with failed ELT due to genetic incompatibility. This is patient's second ELT trial since 2060. High probability that patient is chronically resistant to ELT.*

♎

BODY OF LEARNING HERBAL THERAPY CENTER

Name: *Tamara Fournier*

Your order:

_1_Herbal Longevity Combination Package, $210.00

_1_Mental Acuity Package, $160.00

_1_Perpetual Stamina Package, $190.00

Total so far (before shipping and taxes): *$560.00*

If you order before January 1, 2071, you will qualify for our free shipping discount!

Click *here* to continue.

♎

SCHOLARS' DISTRIBUTION SERVICE, INC.

Article Distribution Order

Order Date: 14-Oct-2075

Name: *Martin Fournier*

Institution: *Providence College*

Office address: *Department of Literature, Providence College, Providence, RI 02918-00011.*

e-mail: *mfournier322@pc.edu*

So far your list contains:

K. Summers, *Rethinking nondiscrimination regulations in the context of the potentials of the Extended Life process*

T. Jenner, *Elizabeth Bennett, Elinor Dashwood and Anne Elliot: models for the 21st-century man?*

P.V. Nomonistan, *Austen's continuing relevance in the atomist theory of literature*

F. Neige, *Each of us left behind: clinical impressions of couples experiencing failure of ELT in one partner.*

S. Renfrew, *Long-term effects of the Extended Life process on population, employment and demographics*

Preferred method of delivery (if you would like different delivery methods for different articles, please complete a separate form for each type of delivery):

___Hardcopy with reproduction rights — $99.99 each

___Hardcopy without reproduction rights — $74.99 each

___Digital with reproduction rights — $49.99 each

_X_ Digital without reproduction rights — $24.99 each

Interstate electronic tax: *$3.75*

Total due: *$128.70*

Charges will be paid by:

___Me (provide credit link *here*)

_X_My institution (provide purchase order link *here*)

♎

MODERN LANGUAGE ASSOCIATION

2090 Annual Meeting

Limited Panel Registration Form

As in previous years, owing to anticipated popularity and limitations on space, certain panel discussions will be attended by reservation only; reservations will be made on a first-come, first-serve basis. Indicate your choice(s) below. We cannot promise to accommodate all preferences.

Name: *Martin Fournier*

Institution: *Providence College*

Limited Panels:

___New theories of the subject: An agenda for research. (Tuesday 9:00 a.m.)

_X_Backlash against Extended Life Recipients in academia and elsewhere. (Tuesday 3:30 p.m.)

___Time to reclaim the middle-class white male? A debate. (Wednesday 10:00 a.m.)

___ELRs: The threat they represent to hiring, promotion and tenure. (Wednesday luncheon)

___Raising the dead? The relevance of Derrida and Foucault in the era of atomist literary theory. (Thursday 9:00 a.m.)

___Stagnation in teaching and research as a result of Extended Lifers in faculty positions. (Thursday luncheon)

♎

PROVIDENCE BILTMORE HOTEL

Banquet/Conference Room Reservation

Today's Date: *January 14, 2091*

Reservation Date: *June 20, 2091*

Reservation Time: *7:00 p.m.*

Reservation Contact: *George Medros, Director, Rhode Island Department of Environmental Management*

Occasion: *Retirement party for Tamara Fournier, Ph.D.*

Number of attendees: *70*

Services included (check all that apply):

__Cash bar

_X_Prepaid bar

_X_Canapés

___Luncheon (attach menu selection page)

___Afternoon tea

_X_Dinner (attach menu selection page)

EXTENDED LIFE ALLIANCE

Rally Against Discrimination

July 4, 2099, starting 11:00 a.m.

The Mall, Washington, D.C.

Yes! I want to prevent unfair laws against the Extended! I will attend the Rally Against Discrimination!

Name: *Martin and Tamara Fournier*

I will (check as many as apply):

_X_Attend the rally.

___Bring snacks or beverages for other marchers.

___Bring signs.

___Link signs.

_X_Call ten people to ask them to attend the rally.

___Organize a bus to transport marchers from my town.

___Write to my Member of Congress and my Senators (see sample letter on next page).

_X_Make a donation of *$500.00* to help fight this discriminatory legislation. (Note that political contributions are not tax-deductible.)

HOWARD UNIVERSITY HOSPITAL

Intake form

Date and time: *7-4-2099 3:35 pm*

Patient name: *Tamara Fournier*

Attending physician: *P. Singh*

Patient age: *78*

History of present illness: *78 year old female presents with coma. Pt collapsed in the Mall approx 2 hrs prior to arrival, witnessed. Pt has not regained consciousness.*

Clinical Impression: *Coma, Heat Stroke*

BIG BROTHERS / BIG SISTERS OF RHODE ISLAND

Receipt for In-Kind Donation

Thank you for your donation! If you itemize the items you have left for us to pick up, we will verify receipt for tax purposes.

Your name: *Martin Fournier*

Date: *9/22/2099*

Items received:

21 women's shirts/blouses

7 women's suits

12 skirts

10 women's pants

17 women's shorts

23 pair women's shoes

11 sweaters

2 women's winter coats

1 women's raincoat

3 women's belts

27 scarves

Please remember that it is your responsibility to determine and verify the monetary value of each of these items for tax purposes. Big Brothers/Big Sisters of Rhode Island makes no assertion as to the market price of any item received.

Verified by stamp: *Big Brothers/Big Sisters of Rhode Island*

PROVIDENCE COLLEGE

Office of Human Resources

Receipt of Severance Payment

Employee Name: *Martin Fournier*

Date of Hire: *September 1, 2053*

Date of Separation: *May 10, 2103*

Reason for Separation:

___Termination for cause

___Resignation

___Retirement

_X_Separation required under Fair Access to Employment Act, 42 U.S.C. § 26000 et. seq.

Amount received: *€649,416.00.*

I hereby acknowledge receipt of the amount specified above, affirm that the amount received above is a fair payment of all debts owed to me by Providence College, and agree to hold the College harmless for any other claims or damages, including, but not limited to, any claims arising out of this separation.

Signed: *Martin Fournier*

FOOD WITHOUT FUSS, LLC

Weekly Order Form

Name: *Martin Fournier*

Order date: *May 21, 2104*

Delivery date: *May 25, 2104*

_X_Home delivery (€70 extra charge).

Include address: *27 Whipple Ave., Barrington*

___In-store pickup

Indicate number of orders (each order serves one person):

Main dishes:

_1_Beef stroganoff over noodles	€164
___Caesar salad	€78
_3_Chicken parmesan with pasta	€155
___Curried shrimp over rice	€140
_1_Fried dumplings (6 pcs)	€94
_3_Pizza with pepperoni	€117
___Tofu stir fry with snow peas and baby corn	€78

Sides:

___Baby carrots (steamed)	€62
___Baked potato	€31
_2_Creamed spinach	€90
_3_French fries	€30
___Side salad	€23

Desserts:

_3_Apple pie	€30
_1_Cheesecake	€35
_3_Chocolate fudge cake	€30

Total food charge:	*€1,395*
Delivery charge:	*€70*
Grand total:	***€1,465***

UNITED STATES DEPARTMENT OF LABOR

Form ELR-3

Last Name: *Fournier* **First Name:** *Martin*
Date DD-MMM-YYYY: *30 Aug 2104*

DOB DD-MMM-YYYY: *24 Sep 2019*

Employer: *University of Connecticut*

Under the Fair Access to Employment Act, 42 U.S.C. § 26000 et. seq., which prevents Extended Life Recipients from monopolizing the labor force, you may not work for this employer unless you sign the following statement and provide supporting documentation to verify its truth.

Under penalties of perjury, I certify that (check one):

___1. I am not an Extended Life Recipient, OR

_X_2. I am an Extended Life Recipient, BUT I qualify for a Hiring Exemption.

If I claim a Hiring Exemption, I certify that I qualify for BOTH an Employer Exemption AND an Industry Exemption (see below).

If I claim an Employer Exemption, I certify that (check one):

_X_3. I have never worked for this Employer before, OR

___4. I first worked for this Employer less than fifty (50) years ago, OR

___5. I last worked for this employer more than (40) years ago.

If I claim an Industry Exemption, I certify that (check one):

___6. This Employer is not in a Protected Industry (see reverse), OR

___7. I have never worked in this Industry before, OR

_X_8. I first worked in this Industry less than seventy (70) years ago, OR

___9. I last worked in this Industry ended more than fifty (50) years ago.

Supporting documentation that you are not an Extended Life Recipient consists of an affidavit, form ELR-7, from a licensed health professional, stating that tests show you do not have Extended Life Markers in your bloodstream.

Supporting documentation concerning the date of your employment with this Employer consists of an affidavit, Form ELR-5, from the most senior human resources officer of the Employer.

Supporting documentation that you have not worked in the relevant Industry for the required time period can be satisfied with a Form ELR-6, to which you must attach a complete résumé. Note: All dates must be accounted for, including all gaps in your employment history.

Signature: *Martin Fournier*

UNIVERSITY OF CONNECTICUT

Student Evaluation of Faculty

Faculty name: *Martin Fournier*

Term: *Spring 2107*

Class: *LIT 4331: The Nineteenth Century English Novel*

Number of forms submitted: *52*

Page 2 — *Text Comments (for numerical summary, see Page 1)*

Not all students submit text comments with their forms. These are all the text comments that appeared in this section.

I liked the course, but I wish the rhetor could have spoken with some expression in his voice.

In general, a good introduction to the subject. But the rhetor seems to think that everything in the 19th century begins and ends with Jane Austen.

Subfrozen. Take the course from someone else. Misplace the monotone, ganger!

Hyperthermal!

Basically hyperthermal, ganger, but misplace all the waxing poetic about Austen.

Subfrozen. Misplace it.

I hype Jane Austen, so I hyped this course. But when you're lecturing about something as beautiful as P&P, couldn't you act as if you're happy about it?

My friends who went to P.C. told me that rhetor Fournier was hyperthermal, but he talks like he's asleep. I wish I'd misplaced it.

UNIVERSITY OF CONNECTICUT

INLINK MEMO

From: Joseph Riccitelli

To: Martin Fournier

Date: April 5, 2107

Re: Course Assignments

I'm sorry, Marty, but I don't think I can accede to your request. First of all, we assign courses on a seniority basis, and you're still relatively low in the hierarchy. We could ask some of the others to trade with you, but I don't think any of them want to teach either 19th BritNov or the Austen course. Secondly, your expertise in Austen and the Romantics was (as you know) one of the primary reasons you were hired in the first place.

Again, sorry. Hopefully you can work your way around this.

Joe

EXTENDED LIFE PAIRING NETWORK

Registration Date: *Jul 4 2109*

Name: *Martin Fournier*

Username: *WidowerProf2019*

Date of Birth: *Sep 24 2019*

Age when received ELT: *40*

(NOTE: The Extended Life Pairing Network is for Extended Lifers only! If you are not an Extended Lifer, please be considerate and do not complete this registration.)

Gender identity:

___Androgynous

___Female

___Genderqueer

___Harmony

___Intersex

_X_Male

___Neutrosis

___Solace

___Transgender

___Transsexual M-to-F

___Transsexual F-to-M

___Other (specify)

___I would rather not say

I would prefer to meet (check all that apply):

___Androgynous

_X_Female

___Genderqueer

___Harmony

___Intersex

___Male

___Neutrosis

___Solace

___Transgender

___Transsexual M-to-F

___Transsexual F-to-M

___Other (specify)

Of the following age (check all that apply):

___25-34

___35-44

___45-54

___55-64

_X_65-74

_X_75-84

_X_85-94

_X_95-104

___105+

Who received their ELT at the following age (check all that apply):

___25-29

___30-34

_X_35-39

_X_40-44

___45-49

Object (check all that apply):

_X_Friendship

_X_Romance

_X_Marriage

___Just sex

_X_Just someone to talk to

What's your EAEA status?

___I'm unemployed.

_X_I won't have to change employers or industries for at least 10 years.

___I'll have to change employers within 10 years, but not industries.

___I'll have to change industries within 10 years.

Complete the 75 Compatibility Criteria below before finalizing registration. Don't forget to include a vid sample!

♎

STATE OF RHODE ISLAND AND PROVIDENCE PLANTATIONS

Marriage License Application

Today's date: *11-8-2112*

Wedding date: *11-15-2112*

Circle Husband or Wife, where appropriate.

Name of *Husband*/Wife 1: *Martin Fournier*

DOB of *Husband*/Wife 1: *9-24-2019*

Has *Husband*/Wife 1 been tested for Extended Life markers?_X_Yes ___No

(Attach physician's certificate to application)

Name of Husband/*Wife* 2: *Melissa Thom*

DOB of Husband/*Wife* 2: *2-3-2033*

Has Husband/*Wife* 2 been tested for Extended Life markers?_X_Yes ___No

(Attach physician's certificate to application)

Note: *While the presence of Extended Life markers does not disqualify you for marriage, you are required to inform your husband/wife of the results of these tests before marrying.*

U. S. INTERNAL REVENUE SERVICE

Form 1040-ELR (2115)

Taxpayer Name(s): *Martin Fournier & Melissa Thom*

To qualify for the ELR Fertility Suppression Tax Credit, check each of the following that apply:

1a. If single, I received the Extended Life Treatment (ELT) before the age of 50. ___

1b. If married, both spouses received the Extended Life Treatment (ELT) before the age of 50. X

If neither line 1a nor line lb is checked, stop here. You do not qualify for the ELRFR Credit.

2a. If single, I received voluntary fertility suppression injections from a qualified physician during 2115. ___

2b. If married, both spouses received voluntary fertility suppression injections from a qualified physician during 2115. X

3. Provide the name(s) and addresses of the physician(s) who administered the fertility suppression injections.

Norma Shok, M.D.
Roger Williams Medical Center
Providence, RI

If neither line 2a nor line 2b is checked, then you do not qualify for the ELRFS Credit.

If you checked either line 1a or line 1b, AND you also checked either line 2a or line 2b, then you qualify for the ELRFS Credit. Write the amount €5,000 (if single) or €10,000 (if married filing jointly) Form 1040, line 75.

FIFTY-FIVE PERCENT FUND

If you believe that U.S. law should no longer disadvantage the 55% of the population who are now Extended Lifers, please consider contributing to our campaign. Every euro will go toward reversing the unfair regulations that still privilege the minority over the majority.

Fight back!

Name: *Martin Fournier and Melissa Thom*

Date: August 8, 2135

Amount contributed:

> ___€500
>
> ___€1,000
>
> ___€2,000
>
> _X_ €4,000
>
> ___Other

♎

SATYAGRAHA CENTER FOR YOGA AND HEALTH

Special Program Registration Form

This offer is being made only to couples who are subscription members of Satyagraha.

Gerianne Komitas, Ph.D., a licensed psychologist and yoga teacher, will give a four-day, three-night workshop on overcoming apathy and malaise for Extended Lifers. Gerianne has counseled dozens of ELP couples, using techniques from meditation, yoga and atmospheric visualization to redirect psychic energies around the sense of wonder, enthusiasm for daily life, passion for professional tasks, and sexual libido that can fade over time in some Extended Lifers.

The workshop will include lectures, visualization and meditation exercises, targeted physical relaxation and concentration techniques, and "homework" assignments for couples to complete in the privacy of their rooms.

Dates are May 3-6, 2140. Space is limited. Rate is €18,999 per couple, including meals and private room.

Names: *Melissa Thom and Martin Fournier*

Address: *33 Tennyson, Johnston, RI*

Email: *mjthom@univmail.net*

♎

NORTHEAST REGIONAL LITERATURE SOCIETY

2147 Annual Meeting

Panel 52 (Thursday, 1:30-3:30): Approaches to pre-Consolidation Anglo-Hegemonic fictive texts

Moderator: E. Nam, Meridan College

S. Lewit, University of Lewiston: *Postatomistic veritropes in Dickens.*

M. Suarez, Colby College Online: *Neorecidivist analysis: should it be limited to post-Consolidation texts?*

A. Temple, Yale-New Haven Polyversity: *Calliopisation characteristic of Fitzgerald, Trollope and Mackenzie-King.*

M. Fournier, Providence College: *Austen on beauty.*

When I first read Kim Stanley Robinson's Green Mars, *I was struck by his suggestion that extended lifespans would allow older workers to keep new entrants out of the market, especially in professions like college teaching. I thought it more likely that we'd see legislation preventing such "unfair" monopolization of the workplace, institutionalizing discrimination against the super-elderly.*

I'm drawn to stories in which the action occurs mostly off-camera and the reader is forced to piece it together, and also to stories where the narrative voice doesn't understand the human drama that is going on. I thought that bureaucratic forms would provide a perfect frame for hiding and displaying a life of passion, heartbreak, loss, and renewal.

— KLS

ABOUT THE AUTHOR

KENNETH SCHNEYER's stories appear in *Analog, Strange Horizons, Beneath Ceaseless Skies, Clockwork Phoenix 3 & 4, Abyss & Apex, Daily Science Fiction, Escape Pod, Podcastle,* and elsewhere, and have been (or soon will be) translated into Russian, Chinese, Spanish and Czech. He attended the Clarion Writers Workshop in 2009 and is a member of the Cambridge Science Fiction Workshop. In 2014, he was nominated for the Nebula Award and was a finalist for the Theodore Sturgeon Memorial Award.

After an almost unmeasurably brief period as an actor, Schneyer worked as a judicial clerk and a corporate lawyer before becoming a professor of legal studies at Johnson & Wales University, where he also teaches the course in science fiction literature. Born in Detroit, he now lives in Rhode Island with one singer, one dancer, one actor, and something with fangs.

LIZ ARGALL is the secret identity of Roller Derby superhero Betsy Nails. Her poetry and prose appear in such places as *Apex Magazine, Strange Horizons, Daily Science Fiction* and *This is How You Die: Stories of the Inscrutable, Infallible, Inescapable Machine of Death.* A native Australian, synthetic Seattleite, Clarion graduate, artists' model, and refuge worker, she also creates the innovative webcomic, *Things Without Arms and Without Legs,* which can be found at www.thingswithout.com

Stillpoint Digital Press

Stillpoint Digital Press creates fine ebook, audiobook, and print editions in genres from fiction to literary nonfiction, from memoir to poetry.

In addition to publishing, Stillpoint provides editing and other publishing services to independent publishers, aiming to give a human face to digital publishing, offering a full range of editorial services, from editing, layout and ebook conversion to distribution and marketing.

For more about Stillpoint Digital Press and its books and services, visit us on the web at **http://stillpointdigitalpress.com**

Made in the USA
Charleston, SC
23 June 2014